AuthorThomasEmry@Gmail.com

Cover art completed by Kelsey Halka | HalkaDesign.com

What Scratches Beneath the Surface. Copyright © 2025 by Thomas Emry

First Edition

All rights reserved.

ISBN13: 979-8-9883136-9-4 (paperback)

ISBN-13: 979-8-9883136-4-9 (hardback)

ISBN-13: 979-8-9883136-3-2 (e-book)

This book is dedicated to Courtney, Colin, and Nolan.
I'm aware I did the same for the last one. Am I supposed to
pick someone else? I don't know. That would feel inaccurate.
Your constant unwavering support means the world to me.

What Scratches Beneath the Surface

Thomas Emry

CHAPTER ONE

"C'mon, we gotta go!" Julie yelled. "They're waiting for us."

Her son shambled into the kitchen. Stephen wore athletic shorts and a hooded Cleveland Browns sweatshirt. At fifteen, his boyish features were melting away, making way for an adult. She stopped what she was doing and looked at him for just a moment.

"You ready?" she asked.

He pulled out one of his earbuds and said, "Huh?"

Julie's whiplash from admiration to annoyance felt all too familiar. His dumb teenager face remained fixed in place as he awaited her response.

"Jesus, I hate those things," she said. "I asked if you're ready. Where's your brother?"

"Yeah, I am. Adam's upstairs, I think. Brushing his teeth or something."

"Adam, let's go!" she yelled. "We're running late!"

Adam poked his head up from the couch in the next room. His shaggy brown hair fell down over his eyebrows. He pushed it aside, and it promptly flopped right back.

"I'm right here," he said. "Why are you yelling at me?"

"Oh, sorry," Julie said, and turned back to Stephen. "Why'd

you tell me he was upstairs?"

He shrugged. "I'm not his keeper."

"Oh, whatever. Get your shoes on. Let's go."

"I haven't eaten anything," Stephen said as he twisted his feet into his already tied sneakers.

"I made you a breakfast burrito. Here." Julie handed him an aluminum foil cylinder.

"I don't like eggs, though," Adam said.

"Yup. I know that, bud. Just sausage and cheese for you," she said, waving a wrapped burrito at Adam and setting it on the counter.

He jogged into the kitchen and grabbed his breakfast. "Isn't Dad coming with us?"

"He's gonna meet us there with the truck. Now let's go." She waved her arms toward the door.

"Why don't we all just ride together?" Stephen asked.

"Because. Now come on. We said we'd be there by nine o'clock to help. We're almost late already. Oh hey, don't you guys still have Connor's game you were supposed to take back to him?"

"Oh, shoot. Yeah. I almost forgot. I'll go grab it," Adam said. With only one shoe on still, he ran to the family room, grabbed the case from the TV stand, and jogged back. "Do you think they'll have the Xbox hooked up yet?"

"They won't have anything hooked up, stupid," Stephen said. "They're not even at the new house yet."

Julie frowned. "Hey! That's enough. Now grab a drink from the fridge and let's go."

They piled into the red Ford Escape and backed to the end of the drive. Julie paused and stared at the pickup truck Wyatt would be following in shortly. As they sat, idling in the driveway, Julie played through all the possible scenarios that lay ahead for them.

"Mom, what are you waiting for?" Stephen asked from the back seat. "No one is coming this way."

Julie shook her head. "Sorry. Thanks, Stephen,"

It was roughly a half-hour drive from their house to Marshport, where they were heading to help the O'Learys move. The two families had been friends since the college days when Wyatt and Phillip lived together off campus.

"Do we gotta help them move every time?" Adam asked.

"Oh, I don't know, bud. What else did you have to do today? Big plans?"

"I don't know. I just wanted to relax, probably."

"Dude, you're a kid. That's all you do is relax," she said, keeping her gaze fixed on the road.

Stephen rolled his eyes. "Ugh, mom. Don't call your kids 'dude'. It's cringy."

She chuckled to herself. "Besides, don't act like you're not going to ditch the adults and hang out with Connor the whole time anyway."

"Yeah, I guess," Adam said.

Three years earlier, Phillip O'Leary had started his own plumbing company, which allowed his wife to work just part-time. This worked great for Corrine, as she regularly jumped from job to job on a whim. It was the only thing she did more often than looking into a new place to live.

The O'Learys had recently signed a lease on a house in the small Ohio town. The house they were leaving, also in Marshport and only a few blocks away from the new one, they'd lived in for barely over a year and a half. Before that, they'd rented a house in Delta for a year after moving from a house in Fremont. Julie often wondered if they were consciously running from something, or if just the thought of familiarity and complacency freaked the hell out of them.

While Julie herself wasn't house hopping or counting two-week-notice and probationary periods, she understood the sentiment.

"Mom, Stephen keeps hitting me!"

"He's wearing those stupid headphones and won't stop

singing," Stephen said. "I can hear it. It's annoying!"

"Oh my god, guys. Just stop. Adam, stop whatever it is you're doing. Stephen, do not put your hands on your brother. You're fifteen years old for Christ's sake. Grow up."

"Yeah, a couple more years and it's assault charges, stupid."

"Shut up, that's not how that works." Stephen looked forward to his mother. "Me grow up? He's still scared of everything. E-very-thing," he repeated.

"Am not!"

"Just stop," Julie said. "I don't want to hear another word until we get there. And then you better get along and be best of friends."

CHAPTER TWO

Phillip grunted as he lifted the box of kitchenware from the grassy front yard.

"Bigger yard is gonna be nice," he said.

"Ooohh, I'm already thinking of all the things I can landscape with," Corrine said. "Home Depot had these ladybug plaques to hang. Oh, oh! And some wind chimes would be amazing. We actually have a porch that I can put them all over now."

"Yeah, yeah. Let's worry about unpacking all the boxes of crap we have now before collecting more."

He stepped into the foyer of 217 Rosemary Drive, eager to soak in the air-conditioning for a brief moment. Connor was frantically opening and closing box flap after box flap in rapid succession.

"Dad, where's the box with the controllers?"

"I don't know. Didn't you label it?"

"No."

"Well, the stuff you didn't pack yourself all got labeled. So, I'd check the boxes that seem like a mystery."

Connor's eyes lit up as he pushed his glasses, which were slightly too big for his face, back up from the tip of his nose.

"Yes!" he said as he spun a box around, examining all sides

of it before moving to the next one.

Phillip dropped the box and wiped his brow, then turned and headed back outside. He stopped at the front step when he noticed Corrine poking around the front yard. As she spun and soaked up the morning sun, her flowy, tie-dyed top waved in the breeze. It was made to be a sundress, but with her tall frame, she wore it as a long blouse over her black leggings.

"Already getting ahead of yourself after all, huh?" he said.

"Never," she said with a smile.

***

Julie grabbed a box marked *Bedroom* out of the back of her SUV. Her navy blue athletic jacket matched the band she wore to keep her ears warm, though it was nearly seventy degrees out, an unusually warm October day. She stopped before heading up to the house and turned to Adam and Stephen, who were still staring at their phones in the back seat.

"Hey, boys, make sure you grab some boxes on your way up to the house. There's plenty back here."

"Okay, Mom," they said in unison.

Julie smiled as she watched Stephen slip his phone into the front pocket of his hoodie, then Adam double-take over at him and follow suit. As she made her way up to the house, Corrine and Phillip were engaged in a playful back-and-forth, picking at each other.

"You leave her be," Julie said. "Whatever she said, I'm on her side."

Phillip threw his hand up in the air. "That figures."

"Oh, hey!" Corrine said, running up to greet Julie. "Sorry I missed you earlier. I had to grab some stuff from Kirk before we— Oh my god, I love that color!" Her eyes zeroed in on Julie's recently dyed red hair.

Julie smirked and raised her shoulders. "Thanks! I don't

know. I'm still getting used to it," she said. "Never gone this far away from blond before."

"Nonsense. You're stunning," said Corrine. "I won't listen to anything otherwise."

Phillip pointed to Julie's headband. "Surely you can't be cold. I'm sweating my ass off out here."

"I just don't like the wind on my ears," she said. "Maybe if I could grow a sweet beard like that, I'd be warmer too."

Adam and Stephen shuffled up to them with moving boxes in their arms. Adam struggled to watch where he was headed, his eyes barely clearing the top of his.

"Oh thanks, guys," Phillip said. "Connor's inside. His room is at the end of that first hallway on the right."

"Cool. Thanks," said Adam. They passed by without stopping, dropped the boxes in stride, and headed off to look for Connor.

The adults watched in slack-jawed amazement at the tunnel vision of the children.

"Where is Wyatt?" Phillip finally said.

Julie looked back down the street. "You know him. He had to double-check every bungee and ratchet strap. He should be pulling up any second."

"We barely left the neighborhood," Corrine said.

Julie shrugged. "Can never be too careful, I guess."

On cue, Wyatt pulled up in front of the house in his rusted green pickup, the dining set and dresser all securely fastened in the truck bed. Heavy metal blared from the cab, allowing the neighbors to hear since all the windows were rolled down. Wyatt smiled at the group on the front lawn.

"You guys waiting for someone?"

"I figured you had to stop halfway and pick all the shit up out of the road with how shoddy everything was secured back there," Phillip said.

"I was actually trying to sell it all to some neighbors along the way, but no one wanted your crap. Come here. Give me a hand."

Wyatt hopped out of the truck as the O'Learys walked up and unfastened the load.

Julie adjusted the box in her arms, which grew heavier by the second. "Let me drop this off real quick, and I'll come help," she hollered. As she started back up toward the house, her husband caught up to her and leaned into her ear.

"You could have at least waited for me," he said.

Julie furrowed her brow and shook her head. "Don't do this now. Please. Let's just help our friends move. We'll talk more later."

Wyatt visibly sank. He pulled off his baseball cap, squeezed and rounded out the bill, then fixed it back atop his head. Julie left him standing in the yard as she entered the house.

The entryway led directly to the family room. A connected hall to the right held the doorways to Connor's bedroom and the bathroom. A small archway bridged the gap into an open over-sized area that served as the kitchen, dining area, and laundry room. Julie walked to a stairway at the far wall of the family room, and placed the box down at the bottom. With no one else around, she let out a stuttered sigh and dabbed her eyes with the cuff of her jacket. From the front window, she watched for a moment as the other three pulled out furniture from back of the truck piece by piece.

She wiped her nose with an old crumpled tissue from her pocket.

"Hold on. I'm coming!" she called out as she jogged out the front door.

Corrine and Julie grabbed a couple of chairs while Wyatt and Phillip carried the kitchen table. After the four brought in the rest of the furniture, they stood catching their breath in the family room. Julie felt Corrine staring at her with eager anticipation.

"So, what do you think?" Corrine asked, bouncing her attention back and forth between Julie and Wyatt.

"I think . . ." Wyatt looked around and scratched the back of his head. "I think it's pretty much the old place. Why'd you move again?"

"No no no," Corrine said as she began prancing around the space to show it off. "The layout may be a bit similar, but the rooms are bigger. Our room and a half bath are upstairs— and secluded." She swayed and winked at Phillip. "It's higher up on the hill so we can see the kids playing at the park. The woods are right there. And this one is right on the river. It's a steal."

"Eh, I'll take your word for it," Wyatt said.

The group froze as a thunderous roar outside grew louder and closer before stopping in front of the house and cutting off entirely. Julie peered out the front door to try and pinpoint the commotion.

"The hell was that?" she asked.

Phillip walked over to the front window and pulled back the curtain. "Oh, it's just Kirk. He said he might stop by."

A few seconds later, a metallic tapping sounded from screen door.

"Knock knock," Kirk said. He stood on the porch, holding a moving box. "May I come in?"

"Of course," Phillip said. "Come on in." He leaned over and held the door open. "You weren't kidding about that muffler. Heard ya coming all the way down the street."

Kirk shuffled by, trying to navigate the box through the door and around Phillip. "Oh yes," he said. "I accidentally hit a darn pothole out in Findlay earlier this week and must have jostled something loose. Anyway, I saw the Jeep still had some boxes in the back and figured I'd make myself useful."

"Here, let me get that." Wyatt put down his drink and grabbed the box from Kirk.

Kirk let go and wiped his hands on the front of his blue jeans. "It was just towels and stuff. But thanks. I'm not as bad off as I seem."

"No worries," Wyatt said. "I've actually got some time after this if you want us to look at that while you're here."

"No, no. You all have enough going on. I'm finally getting around to calling for an appointment on Monday. No, I just wanted to check in and see how you kids were doing."

Julie let out an involuntary chuckle. Kids? He looked to be only around ten or fifteen years older than the rest of them, though his clothes, and the way he walked—slightly hunched and favoring his left side—gave him the appearance of someone much older.

"Julie, Wyatt, I don't know if you guys have met Kirk," said Corrine. "He owns the house. Well, houses. We just transitioned the old lease."

"Yes, we found an opportunity that worked out for both of us," Kirk added.

Wyatt nodded. "Yeah, I think we've met. Probably at the other place or something." He grabbed a drink from his cooler and pointed it at Kirk. "Beer?"

Kirk waved it off. "Oh, no thank you. I'm going to be in and out. Just checking on how things are going, and let these guys know I'll be over tomorrow to replace the broken trim in the hallway."

"Sounds good. Thanks. I think we should be able to get everything moved over today," said Phillip. "Spend tomorrow cleaning up the old place for ya."

"Toothpasting the nail holes and replacing the cracked switch plate in the kitchen?" Kirk said, smiling.

"Yeah, something like that."

"I've been at this a long time and seen it all. I could tell you stories," Kirk said. "Lot of history in this town. Maybe one day I'll come and bore you with it all. In fact, this very house used to be one of the central spots, way back when it was a bar."

"It's not boring one bit," Corrine said. "There's not many places like this anymore. I just love it. The vibes. The charm.

The community." She brought her cup of tea to her face with both hands and breathed in the passion fruit aromatics. Strong —Julie could smell it from where she stood. Corrine shook out her shoulders and appeared to melt into herself.

"And we can't wait to finally get you more involved in the community," Kirk said. "We all have our place in how it runs. The Marshport way of life is something the bigger cities could only hope to achieve. I feel like, with your spirit, Marshport will stay in good graces for a long time to come. That old house was almost on the outskirts of town. You'll feel much more included here. Right in the mix of everything. Ooh, you could start by joining us for church this Sunday. New beginnings are a great time to get right with the Lord."

"Eh, Kirk, again, we will have to respectfully decline," Phillip said.

The man sank a little. His frown, compounded with his hunched lean, made him appear almost desperate.

"And what about you all?" he asked Wyatt. "There's always room in the pews for new people."

Wyatt choked on his beer and sat up straight.

"Oh— No. Thank you," he said. "Not really our thing."

Kirk looked further dismayed and shook his head. "No worries. There were a few other small boxes I can go grab."

As he walked back outside, Wyatt turned to Phillip. "I think we just ruined his day. Where the hell did that come from?"

"Oh, he's fine," Corrine said. "He's not hurting anybody by asking. Who knows. Maybe you could learn a little from him about being devout."

Phillip stared out the window as Kirk went out for more boxes. "I'm gonna go give him a hand. Devout or not, if he falls, he's gonna raise our rent to cover medical expenses."

Julie rolled her eyes. "I don't think that's how that—"

Adam sprinted down the hall and right up to his mother, short of breath and gleaming. The other two boys stood at the end of the hallway, watching.

"Mom, can we stay the night?"

Not wanting to immediately be the bad guy, Julie looked around to Wyatt and Corrine for some kind of feedback, but they were of no immediate assistance.

"Oh, I don't know, bud," she said. "They've had a big day and still have a lot of work to do."

"Actually, it's fine with me, if you don't care," Corrine said. "Encouraged, even. It'll give Connor something to do while Phillip and I are unpacking tonight."

"And while Corrine goes round and round with herself about how she wants the furniture arranged," Wyatt said, promptly receiving a mocking glance from her.

"I mean, yeah, if it's okay with you," Julie said. "They don't have anything with them."

Wyatt nodded. "And if they did, they wouldn't use it anyway."

"Yeah. That's true, I guess," Julie said, defeated.

"Cool!" Connor said. "I got all the game boxes in my room. Let's go set them up!"

The three boys ran off down the hall to his room.

"Corrine, if you change your mind, feel free to call," Julie said.

"Ah, I probably won't even see them all night."

CHAPTER THREE

As Phillip and Corrine shifted the TV stand, chairs, and coffee table in a myriad of positions around the family room, they listened to the sounds of the boys running and laughing paired with the firing of dart guns. Though they attempted to sneak around, the trio were somehow louder than if they'd just run freely throughout the house.

Corrine turned the coffee table parallel to the couch. She took two steps back, examined it, and shook her head before rotating it the opposite way and sliding it to the middle of the room.

"Why can't we just set it up how we did before?" Phillip said. "You'd still have more room."

"Oh, you're boring," she said. "You have to take into account the glare from the window, walking space around everything, where the plants are going to get the most sunlight. Don't worry, just keep looking cute and move the bookcase over into that corner. I need to see if it feels right."

He rolled his eyes at her, and Corrine blew him a kiss. She whipped around toward the hallway at the sound of Stephen running into the living room. Before she could tell him to slow down, he tripped over and toppled an end table, landing intertwined in its legs.

"Dammit, Stephen!" Corrine said, more startled than frustrated. "You okay? You gotta be careful."

"Yep, I'm good," he said. He climbed back up to his feet and stood the table back up. "Sorry, Corrine."

"Give me the gun," she said.

Stephen looked at the floor, then back up to her. He handed over the Nerf rifle. Corrine narrowed her eyes, then slowly cracked, letting a smile spread across her face.

"Now run," she said, cocking back the gun.

Stephen spun on his heel and ran the other way. He narrowly dodged a dart that whizzed by his ear, then ran into Connor, causing them both to fall over. They laughed on the ground as Connor rubbed his head. Stephen checked the elbow he'd banged against the wall. They must have agreed their war wounds weren't life-threatening, because they both ran on four legs toward more artillery at the end of the hall. Corrine laughed and turned back to the furniture.

***

Adam, with his orange-and-yellow shotgun cocked and ready, sat in the bathroom waiting for his opportunity. As the other two boys scurried by, he fired. One shot hit Stephen as he ran from the open fire of the living room. Adam giggled and moved from the bathroom to the hall closet, where he reloaded in his new cover spot.

He sat low, with his legs folded. The closet, still empty except for Adam himself, felt massive, no linens or cleaning supplies or bedding inside yet. In the heat of the moment, he didn't even notice the space. Or how dark it was. All he noticed was how cold it felt.

Inside the dark, vacant space, Adam sat and shivered. The chilled air brushed against his neck, as he tried his best to pretend it wasn't there. But it was all he could focus on. His mind flooded with dread as the showdown on the other side of the door drifted farther and farther away, until finally fading into the vacuum of space. The only thing left in the world was Adam. He fell deeper and deeper into the sensory deprivation of the hall closet in his best friend's new house. He sat immobile, unable to move even if he wanted, other than the involuntary tremble of his teeth chattering. As he sank deeper into himself, and the echoes of his own stunted breathing reverberated louder and louder, the hallway door swung open.

"Adam!" Phillip said. "There you are. You didn't hear us calling you?"

"Jeez," Corrine said. "You sure know how to hunker down. Come on. Let's get these darts all cleaned up."

Adam climbed back up to his feet and emerged into the hallway.

"Oh, dude. You okay? You're super pale," Stephen said. "Looks like you saw a ghost."

Without answering, Adam slid past them and crawled into the sleeping bag on the floor next to Connor's bed. As he lay there, he rocked on his side. Someone nudged him with their foot.

"Hey, man. You good?" Connor asked.

"Yeah. I'm fine," he said. His arm was still littered with goosebumps. "Just got tired."

"Okay, we'll be in in a minute."

On the floor, with the top of the sleeping bag clenched in his grasp just above his chin, Adam listened to the others in the family room. They laughed and joked without care, until everything slowly faded away.

***

Adam awoke unsure of the time, or how long he had been sleeping. The bedroom door was closed. The green LED glow of the computer base offered a soft light, revealing the other two boys now in the room with him. He tried to ignore the urge and go back to sleep, but couldn't. He had to pee. Badly.

He opened the door and peeked out just enough to see down the hallway. The late-night shadows made the passage seem much longer now than when he'd fired darts down it only a few hours ago.

Adam held his breath and crept past the hallway closet, making his way to the bathroom. He closed the door behind him and rested his back against the sanctuary wall. He did his business and washed his hands, but hesitated when it was time to head back. His sweaty palms were cold and clammy. He bounced up and down, charging up the necessary courage.

Holding his breath again, he stared at the floor and made a beeline for Connor's room. Sprinting full force, with his eyes on the ground, something along the wall snagged his leg and he fell. He let out a whimper as the breath leapt from his chest. Without looking back to locate what had tripped him, he continued the rest of the way on all fours, not stopping until he crossed the threshold of the bedroom. Adam collapsed, his heart thumping, and closed the door behind him. He rolled over to the sleeping bag, burrowed inside, and stayed there until morning.

CHAPTER FOUR

Julie raised her fist to knock on the door. Before she connected, it flung open and Adam wrapped his arms around her.

"Oh hey, bud!" She used her free hand, the one not holding a travel mug, to hug him back. "Good morning! You have fun?"

He answered without words by squeezing harder. With his head down, and shuffling his feet, he walked to the SUV and climbed into the back seat.

"Uh . . . okay. I guess we're just gonna head out," Julie said. She looked up at Corrine. "What was that about?"

"Not sure. He's been pretty quiet this morning. I figured they just stayed up too late or something. He ate some cereal when he got up."

"Weird. Okay. Stephen, you ready?" she yelled down the hall. "Your brother's already in the car!"

Stephen and Connor appeared from around the corner of the hallway before she finished her sentence.

"God, Mom. I'm right here. Why are you yelling?"

"Well, for all I knew you were still zoned out killing aliens in Call of Duty or something."

Stephen rolled his eyes and turned to Connor. "All right

man, I'll see ya."

"Yeah. Later."

"You thank Corrine for letting you stay?" Julie asked.

"Thanks, Corrine," Stephen said.

"Of course! Anytime."

Julie mussed Stephen's hair as he walked by. She smiled at Corrine.

"Connor, come here a sec," she said. "Just because I don't want you to think less of me, I need you to know I know exactly what Call of Duty is. I just like to mess with my kids."

Connor looked at Julie, chuckled, and looked back down at his feet.

"I'm gonna wear you down eventually," she said. "You'll come around and love me. Bye, Corrine. Thanks for keeping them."

Julie jogged out to the car, trying and failing to dodge the drizzle that had started in her short time inside. She slid into the driver's seat and looked back.

"You guys have fun?" she asked as she pulled out of the driveway.

"Yeah, it was cool," Stephen said, not looking up from his phone.

Adam remained quiet, staring out of the window. He focused on the drops of rain as they raced from the top of the glass down to the bottom edge. When they returned home, he retreated straight to his room.

As Stephen opened the fridge to grab something to drink, Julie stopped him.

"Hey, Stephen. Did anything happen last night? To Adam, I mean."

"No," he said, then took a second to think about it. "No, we had a dart gun war, played some games, it was pretty chill. Why?"

"You don't think he's acting weird?"

"I always think he's acting weird."

"Ugh, never mind. Go."

***

Julie didn't say anything to Wyatt about Adam's behavior. She didn't say much to Wyatt in general. Outside of therapy, the two barely spoke at all. Subconsciously, maybe, it was their way to avoid fighting in front of the children while they worked out their issues.

The night before helping the O'Learys move, they had argued late into the night. Like usual, it started over something trivial. But it ended with Julie telling Wyatt she didn't see an outcome where they remained happy in their marriage. It was the last real conversation they'd had. Even last night, with no children on a Saturday night, they'd gone their separate ways.

Tonight, at the dinner table, they attempted to put on a brave face and make nice. Partly to hide their rift from the children. Partly to see if there really was anything worth salvaging. Coexisting was easier with the children nearby to act as a buffer or a sounding board.

"The yard looks nice, Stephen," Wyatt said. "Thanks for getting it cut today."

"Yeah, no problem."

"Hopefully it's the last time it needs done," Julie said. "I'm ready to decorate for Halloween."

"Me too. The Foleys have had their stuff up for weeks," Wyatt said.

"Yeah, but they give out Twizzlers every year," Stephen said. "They kinda suck."

"Stephen, that's not nice." Julie offered him a smile. "Even if it's absolutely true."

Stephen laughed and took another bite of food.

"So, boys, how was the new house?" Wyatt asked.

Stephen shrugged. "It was fine."

Adam stared in a trance at his plate, moving the food around with his fork.

"Adam, you okay? You barely touched your dinner," said Wyatt.

He sighed. "I don't want to stay the night there again. I don't like their house."

Julie froze as the day replayed in strobed flashes. She'd known there was something up. Wyatt crinkled his eyebrows at her, and they both turned back to Adam, who still hadn't looked up from his dinner plate. It wasn't what he'd said that unnerved Julie as much as the nonchalant delivery with which the words filled the air. The way someone would ask to pass the butter or talk about the weather.

"Why? Did something happen?" Wyatt asked. "You get in a fight with Connor again?"

"No. He was cool."

"Did Phillip get after you about something?"

"No. I don't like their house."

"Their house?" Julie said. "It's basically the same as the old one."

"Some would wonder why they even moved at all," Wyatt added.

Julie shot him a look, which he only smiled at, taking another bite of food.

"I heard stuff. And the closet was cold. And I had to go the bathroom at night, and something grabbed me and made me fall."

Julie's mind flooded with questions about why he'd kept this to himself all day. But all she got out was, "What do you mean something grabbed you?"

"My pant leg. And I fell. It grabbed me."

Her attention flipped to Wyatt, and they traded confused yet concerned looks.

"I knew you wouldn't believe me." Adam shrank in his

chair.

"Of course we believe you, bud," Wyatt said. "Are you okay? I'll call Phillip after dinner and ask about it."

Julie slid her arm across the table toward Adam, who sat slightly out of reach. "Yeah, and you don't have to go anywhere you don't want to. Of course."

***

As the phone rang, Julie didn't know whether to get right into it or casually mention the conversation at dinner. She didn't fully decide until realizing she'd hung up without actually getting to the point.

"Hey, Corrine," she said.

"Julie, what's up? One of the boys forget something?"

"No, nothing like that. Hey, I know I asked when I picked them up earlier. But, um, did anything weird happen? Adam's been, well, he's been off all day."

"Not really. I think he got upset last night with the other boys about something. But he didn't mention it. When I asked him, he said he was fine. He went to bed early, though. I asked Connor and Stephen if they said anything to hurt his feelings, but they said no. I kind of just wrote it off as him having a big day with the moving and stuff. Did he say something?"

"No. Well . . ." She ran through a hundred variations of There's something in the closet that grabbed me, none of which sounded right. "Can I come over tomorrow? I've got some errands to run and want to see the new place now that it's all put together."

"Of course. Sounds great."

***

As Julie stood at the bathroom mirror and performed her

nightly facial routine, she glanced over at Wyatt. Tethered to the wall by a charger, he lay in bed and stared up at his phone, entranced by what sounded like a YouTube video on how to smoke the most mouthwatering burnt ends.

"Hey, what did Phillip say when you asked about what Adam said?" she asked.

"Oh, shit. I forgot all about it."

She rolled her eyes as she rubbed in the moisturizer across her forehead.

"I figured as much. Don't worry about it, I guess."

"Sorry. I really was. It just slipped my mind after dinner."

"No, really. I'm going to go talk to Corrine tomorrow."

"Oh, okay. What did she say when you asked her about it?"

"I sort of decided last minute to talk to her in person. Seemed best."

Wyatt fumbled his phone, almost dropping it onto his face.

"Oh, God. I can only imagine what she's going to say."

Julie chuckled as she slipped into bed.

"Oh, stop. She keeps things . . . interesting."

"That's a word for it I guess," he said.

She started to put on her sleeping mask but stopped when she noticed Wyatt still looking at her.

"What?"

"Nothing," he said. He grabbed a strand of her hair and tucked it behind her ear. "I do like the red. Sorry if I didn't say anything before. You got a Jessica Rabbit vibe going on."

She smiled. "Thanks. Me too." She slipped the mask over her face, only to lift one side so she could peer out at him with one eye. "And I always did have a weird crush on Roger Rabbit growing up."

CHAPTER FIVE

The drive to Marshport looked like most drives through Ohio when not traveling in one of the few bigger cities. An equal mix of grayscale industrial areas, train yards with crossings six or seven tracks deep, and cornfields that spanned beyond the horizon. This time of year, the crops stood tall at attention and swayed in the morning breeze. It wasn't until Julie reached Marshport itself that anything had any identifying characteristics at all.

The sign at the end of the bridge coming over the river greeted her in detailed glamour. *Welcome to Marshport est. 1863.* It arched over the bridge, swallowing her in the small-town charm as she entered. The town lettering was bold, but without sharp edges. The rest of the words flowed in a wraparound cursive style. Julie didn't recognize any of the buildings or people on the sign, but assumed they were important in their own way. She wondered if every road into the town held the same pomp and circumstance.

When Julie arrived, Corrine already had water boiling for tea.

"What do we have today?" Julie asked.

"Oooh, I just got this great pomegranate black tea. It is amazing. You have to try it. I'll send you home some."

"Sounds perfect," Julie said, and followed Corrine into the kitchen.

Corrine opened the flaps of a cardboard box on the counter, shook her head, and closed it back up. She moved on to another. "Ahh, here we go," she said, pulling out two ceramic floral mugs. "Sorry. Still living out of moving boxes a bit."

"I get it. Are you doing it all yourself?"

"Well, Phillip helped me most of yesterday with moving the bigger furniture around. But yeah, pretty much. He was supposed to block out a few days on his work calendar, but he's also freaking out a bit about the new lease. It's a little bit more, and should be well within our budget, but he's stressed for sure. Won't admit it. Just keeps saying dumb shit like 'gotta keep grinding,' like a giant douchebag. God love him."

She looked inside one of the mugs, scrunched her face, and wiped it out with a rag before adding the bag and boiling water. "So, how are things with you and Wyatt?" Corrine asked as she sat down and slid the tea over to Julie.

Julie's face deadened, and she stared down at her drink. "Is it that obvious?"

"Your energy is off today. I figured that's what really brought you over. You're worried about something."

"Oh, it's not— I mean— Ugh. I don't know," Julie said, starting in protest but giving in to shifting gears. "We're trying, I guess? It's been tough. We're both spread so thin. It's funny, because it's not like we hate each other, ya know? We can sit there and have great days where everything seems fine. Then others . . . I don't know. It's like the smallest thing sets us off." She looked down and tapped the side of her mug. "We talked about separating."

"Oh, Jules, are you okay? I'm so sorry. I didn't realize it was that bad."

Julie looked up at her friend, then right back down to her drink. "Well, I talked about separating. He wasn't so keen on it."

"You guys barely spoke on moving day," Corrine said.

She shook her head. "God, really? We tried to get along and get through the day. I'm sorry."

"Don't be." The concern on Corrine's face shifted to a small smirk. "I don't think Phillip noticed anything, if it makes you feel better. Shocker. Do the boys know?"

"I don't think so. They're off in their own worlds. The teenager and the preteen going on senior citizen."

Julie and Corrine both laughed, and Julie rubbed her hands back and forth on her thighs. "So, not to change the subject away from me oversharing, but I have to ask one more time. Because Adam was upset after we left yesterday. You sure nothing happened?"

"Really? No, we unpacked. The boys played games. All pretty straightforward. I can talk to Connor again when he gets home from school just to make sure."

"He said something about a closet," Julie said.

"Oh," Corrine said. Her tone shifted like something had finally clicked. "I don't . . . Oh . . . well, yeah, I guess when we were all shooting darts at each other, he hid in the hall closet. He didn't come out right away. But he went to bed soon after that. Like I said, I thought one of the other boys said something to upset him. You know how his feelings get hurt. Why? Did he see something?"

"Corrine?" Julie put her mug down and leaned forward. "What do you mean 'see something'?"

"I mean, it's probably nothing," she said.

"Corrine. What closet?"

She stood up and walked Julie to the hallway. Corrine turned the knob and gave it a hearty tug, opening the door.

"It sticks," she said. "Old house."

Julie wasn't sure what she'd expected to see. But given Corrine's ominous demeanor, it surprised her to find the inside rather ordinary. Some bath towels on the shelf, toiletries, and the like. A vacuum cleaner with the cord wrapped tightly around it. The closet was, however, noticeably colder.

"Crawlspace entrance or something?" she asked.

"No crawlspace."

"It's cold in there."

"Okay, look. I guess there is something I should tell you," Corrine said. Her defensive reaction came in short rapid bursts. "I wasn't gonna bring it up because I knew how you'd react. The people who lived here before us . . . their little girl died in the house. The closet shelves, like, basically fell on top of her or something. She was about ten, I guess? That's what Kirk told me."

"What the hell, Corrine!"

"I know! I wasn't even going to say anything about it because I knew you'd freak out. It was years ago. But that's probably what—"

"What the fuck? You knew this ahead of time?"

"Yeah. He went over the whole thing with me."

"And you let my kids stay here?"

"My whole family lives here. There's nothing wrong. I thought you didn't believe in that stuff anyway."

"I don't. But . . ." Julie had no response. She searched the hallway for words, finding nothing. She finally mustered up a repeat of, "It's cold."

"I know. I haven't seen her. If that's what you're getting at."

"I wasn't. But is that why it was vacant?"

"Not sure. Maybe," Corrine said.

"I don't know. How can you live in a house like that?"

"Like what?" Corrine asked. "The poor girl wasn't killed. It was an accident. Tragic, yes. But it's not a murder house or anything."

"It just seems . . ." Julie rubbed her eyes with her palms as her thought trailed off. "I don't know."

"What do you want me to say? I saged the house. I haven't

felt any negative energy. I did a full walk-through before signing the papers." As Corrine spoke, her hand gestures grew increasingly animated. "People die, Jules. Not to sound morbid. If you're never going to live in a house where someone died, you'll have to just build your own. I don't know about you, but I don't have that kind of money. But if you focus on the energy you expel into the universe, it shines back onto you."

"That's such . . ." Julie groaned and let out an aggravated chuckle. "I can't believe you."

"I'm sorry. I didn't think it would ever come up. At least not right away. Is he okay? Like, did he see anything?"

"He said something grabbed him. But if he saw anything, he didn't mention it." Julie shook her head. She pulled the door open further and looked around the closet more closely. "Adam says he doesn't want to come over anymore, so there's that."

"He never even mentioned anything when he was here," Corrine said, sounding equally sincere and hurt.

"I'll talk to him today. See if I can pull anything out of him." Julie sighed and rubbed her eyes. "He's already got that teenager attitude. He's only eleven. God help me."

CHAPTER SIX

When Adam arrived home from school, Julie intercepted him at the door.

"Hey, bud. How was your day?"

"Good," he said as he kicked off his shoes.

"What'd you do in school?"

Adam shrugged. "Nothin' really."

"Nothing all day? Why am I even sending you? Just drop out."

"Can I?" he said, finally perking up and looking at her.

"No. Hey, I wanted to talk to you more about when you went to Connor's house."

"Why?"

"Oh, I was just thinking about what you said. About not wanting to go over there."

"Oh my god. Mom, I'm fine. Just forget I said anything."

"No, I know, I know. It's just, I talked to Corrine and—" She paused. As she looked at Adam, she wondered whether it was wise to even bring it up. He hadn't mentioned it again, even with her repeatedly poking him about it. "She was hoping you're okay."

"Yeah. I'm good. Stephen said my mind was playing tricks on me. I talked to Connor today, actually. He's getting the new zombie DLC. I want to go over there this weekend."

Julie chuckled in disbelief. "Really?"

"Yeah, of course!"

Maybe it truly had just been some jitters, she thought. That was perfectly normal.

"All right, if you're sure. I'll double-check with everything, but it should be fine. I don't think we have anything going on."

"Sweet!" he said. "You gotta come too, though. Remember, I don't want to stay!" he added before running off to his room.

She stood there for a moment, stunned.

"Hey, hey, wait! Come back here!" she yelled. "What's going on now? I'm confused."

He turned around and started back. "I want to go hang out, but I don't want to stay. So we're going over there for dinner on Saturday."

"Said who? I just talked to Corrine today."

Adam looked up at his mother like she was asking the obvious. "Connor and I planned it. His mom knows. They're grilling out."

"Hold on. That's all well and good for you and Connor, but the adults need to talk before you get to plan anything."

"Okay. You should go call her."

"Excuse you?"

"I mean, please . . . can you go call her?"

She turned to walk away, then stopped and faced him again. "You're sure? Because just yesterday—"

"Yes. I'm sure. I swear. Can we go?"

"Just . . . just let me talk to her."

***

Wyatt arrived home shortly after. He placed his lunchbox and coffee thermos on the counter and marched straight to the refrigerator.

"Hey," he said as he reached in and grabbed a beer.

"Hey," Julie said. She glanced up, then back down to the chicken alfredo she was folding together. "You're home late."

"Oh, please don't even start. I'm not in the mood."

"I'm not starting anything. Really. Shitty day?"

He smiled as if to say "you have no idea" as he shook his head.

"You want one?" he asked, offering her a bottle.

"Sure. You want to talk about it?"

"Not really. I just want to not think about work. Or anything for that matter."

He folded his arms on the kitchen counter and bent over, stretching and extending his back.

"Oh, Saturday we're going to go to Corrine and Phillip's for dinner."

He stood back up and spun around. "This Saturday?" he said.

"Yeah. Why?"

"We have reservations for dinner on Saturday. Second Saturday of the month, remember?"

"Shit! I forgot. Well, we can do it next weekend."

"That's not how this works. We need to prioritize each other. Remember? It can't be next weekend, anyway. I'm on call."

"Well, I don't know, Wyatt. Maybe we just skip this one. There's a good reas—"

"Make time for each other. Remember? We agreed. I'm trying here, Jules. But I can't be the only one. It's getting fucking exhausting."

"It's not like that this time. Maybe we can do both. Go over early?"

Wyatt took another swig from his beer and turned to leave the room.

"Do whatever the fuck you want," he said.

"Oh, real mature," Julie said. "Just walk away like normal.

Maybe if you asked me about my fucking day, you'd know why we're even going over there."

As Wyatt left the kitchen, Adam emerged from the dark living room. Wyatt scratched the top of his head. "Hey, bud."

"Hey," he said. Adam crept up to the stove beside his mother. "Hey, Mom?"

Julie spun away so he couldn't see her face as she regained her composure.

"Yeah, buddy, what's up?"

"My homework is done. Do I have time to play a game before dinner?"

"No, not really. We're eating in about ten minutes."

"Okay. After dinner?"

"Y-yeah," she said, stuttering as her voice cracked.

Adam wrapped his arms around her. "I love you," he said.

***

Setting the table and eating as a family was a regular ritual for them when they could, when there were no bowling nights or martial arts classes or any other evening activities acting as a distraction to spread families too thin.

Julie smiled at Stephen as she handed him a stack of dinner plates. Adam took a handful of silverware from the drawer. Wyatt carried the pot of pasta, and Julie watched him wait patiently for her to drop a hot pad for him to set it on. After placing it down, she glanced up at him, finally noticing him looking at her with apologetic eyes. She rubbed his arm, and he pulled her in close.

As they ate, Julie floated around in her head about how to make the weekend work. And if she even wanted to exhaust the effort.

"Stephen," she finally said, "we'll need you to watch your brother this weekend after getting back from Connor's. Your dad and I are going out."

"I can't. I've got Ross's birthday on Saturday. You're supposed to drop me off for paintball, and I'm staying with him."

Julie and Wyatt shot an "oh shit, I forgot" look at each other.

"You guys forgot. Didn't you?" Stephen said.

"No," Wyatt said. "Your mom was just saying earlier how we still needed to get a gift for him."

Stephen sat up straight and wiped his mouth on a napkin. "Nice try."

"Didn't work at all?" Wyatt asked.

"Not even close."

"Well, that's fine," Julie said. "We'll make it work." She turned to Wyatt. "Maybe your sister can watch Adam."

"Out of town this weekend. Dance recitals for Brie in Columbus."

Adam looked back and forth between his parents. "Maybe I can just stay at Connor's after you leave."

"No, no. We will figure something out," Julie said.

"It's cool. Really."

"I think it'd be good for him," Stephen said.

"Oh, what do you know?" Adam shot back.

"Whoa whoa whoa," Stephen said. "So hostile. Mom, your son is getting mouthy. Puberty, amiright?"

"Boys, stop," Wyatt said.

"Well, I mean yeah, I guess. Let me make sure it's okay with them. Is that what you want to do? You're sure?" Julie asked.

Adam nodded. "Yeah."

***

Wyatt and Julie cleaned up dinner together, physically working around each other but not really in the same space. The day had tapped Julie out emotionally, leaving little energy to try and navigate the minefield of a conversation. She didn't have to ask Wyatt to know he felt the same. The kitchen air thickened around them. A familiar feeling she couldn't pinpoint, but one of the only things they agreed on anymore was how uncomfortable they felt traversing their own home.

"Wyatt, we need to talk about this weekend," Julie said, finally cracking the seal. "We should find somewhere else to take Adam. Or postpone. I don't feel great about him staying over there."

"At Phillip and Corrine's? Since when?"

"Are you serious? Since the last time, when he was so scared. You weren't there to pick him up. He practically ran out of the house. He says he's fine now, but . . . I don't know."

"Oh c'mon, Jules. That's just how he is. We go through this all the time. Remember when he was at my mom's house and wanted to come home, said there was nothing to do? Then we come to find out he had a great time making cookies and watching old movies. We had to go buy the Back to the Future box set afterward because he was obsessed. He gets something in him sometimes where he just wants to be home. And he's stubborn about it. I get it, but he can't be that way all the time. You said yourself that he's wanted to be picked up late at night a few times now. Sometimes, he just needs to stick it out. I don't know if you've noticed, but he doesn't really have a lot of friends. What's going to happen if he stops going over there?"

"Wyatt, they think there's a ghost," she blurted out, and immediately froze as she realized the absurdity.

Her husband stopped drying dishes and pivoted toward her. "Are you kidding me right now?"

"Corrine thinks that's what frightened Adam."

"Is that what she said? A ghost scared our kid?"

"Not exactly. But there was a girl, and the closet that he mentioned being scared of—she had an accident. And it's cold in there." She trailed off, grasping what she was actually saying.

"Julie, ignoring the fact that Corrine's kind of a whack job, and you don't even believe in that shit . . . the closet is cold? Is that what we're basing all this on? Have TVs been turning on randomly? Chairs flying all over the place on their own? Walls bleeding? C'mon. They live next to the fucking river. Their whole house is probably drafty as hell. What is this about?"

"I—"

"Do you honestly just not want to try? Is that what it is? Are you looking for any excuse not to be alone together? That's what it seems like, because now you're being elaborate about it."

"That's not it. The little girl died in the house."

"And that's heartbreaking, but for fuck's sake. Our house was built in the sixties. You think nobody passed away who lived here? Look, I . . . I want us to work through . . . whatever you want to call this. I really do. I've avoided the subject since you said it, hoping it was just one of those heat-of-the-moment things where you say stuff you don't mean. But it has been eating away at me for days. I don't want to throw it all away. I don't say it enough probably, but I still love you. More than anything."

"Me too." She winced and rubbed her temples. "Look, okay, I don't feel good about it. But you're right. We're going over there that afternoon. We already decided that. If we change our mind, we can bring him back home. He can stay here alone or something. I don't like that at all either, but I can keep checking up on him or something."

"Deal. If anyone gets possessed, I won't leave my son at their house anymore."

***

Adam gently knocked on Stephen's bedroom door, then opened it wide enough to slide his head inside.

"Hey, can I come in?"

"Yeah, that's fine," Stephen said. He sat at the end of his bed, answering without breaking eye contact with his videogame.

"Hey, can—"

"Hold up," Stephen said.

"Okay."

Adam wandered around the room, examining the martial arts trophies and band posters. Though they got along well enough most of the time, Adam still felt extremely nervous whenever he needed to ask his brother for a favor. Like he'd accidentally sign himself up to be indebted for life. He picked up one of his brother's sais from a display stand on the dresser and moved it back and forth, watching the light glare dance across the metal.

"I'm so jealous," he said while waving it around. "These are so cool. I'm thinking of quitting soccer and picking up karate." He stuck his fingers between the prongs of the sai and began stabbing the air.

"Yeah, that's coo— Hey, don't mess with those. You don't even know what you're doing."

"What, I'm not gonna really hit anything. Besides, you said you were going to teach me. And you never did."

Stephen smiled. He paused the game and hopped off the foot of the bed.

"Okay, well for one, you're holding them wrong. Here, hold them up. Try and block this." Stephen looked around the room for something to use and eventually grabbed a drumstick off the set in the corner. "You ready?" he said, and swung down.

Adam put the sai up to block it, and the drumstick smacked against his knuckle between the prongs.

"Ow! What'd you do that for?"

"I told you. You're holding 'em wrong. Those were used to

defend against swords and stuff. You're not supposed to put your fingers in there."

"That's what Raph does."

"That's because the ninja turtles were made by two dudes from New England. Not actual martial artists, dork."

"And Elektra."

"Same thing, different guy."

"Ow. It still hurts," Adam said, blowing on his knuckles to heal the wounds. "And don't call me a dork. Do you even know what that is?"

"You'll be fine." Stephen sat back down and picked up the controller.

"So, hey, can you please come to Connor's with me on Saturday?" Adam asked. "I only said I wanted to in the first place because I thought we'd both be there."

"I can't. I'm hanging out with Ross that night. If you don't want to go, just tell Mom and Dad."

"No. Mom and Dad are actually going out. I don't want to ruin it. They try to hide it, but they fight all the time."

"What?" Stephen scoffed. "No, they don't. Stop lying."

"Yeah, they do! I'm not lying! Pay the hell attention," he said clenching his fists. "You're always in here. You never know what's going on!"

Stephen glanced back at his brother, then back to the TV. "Okay. Okay," he said, smiling to himself. "No need for foul language, big guy."

"Whatever. C'mon. Please. I'll do your chores for a week."

"Nope. Sorry."

"Maybe I can come with you guys then. Your karate friends like me."

"It's MMA. Not karate. And I'm not babysitting."

"Please."

"No, Adam. Jesus, stop begging. You sound like a baby."

"Whatever. You suck!" Adam said, and slammed the door behind him on the way out.

CHAPTER SEVEN

"You already rearranged again," Julie said. She examined the O'Learys' living room in amazed disbelief. "I was just here earlier this week."

Corrine beamed. "Don't you love it? The whole room just flows now."

"Yeah, it's very, uh . . ." Wyatt looked around. "Yeah, I got nothin'. Phil, help me out here."

"No life raft from me, dude. Have fun drowning."

In the living room, Phillip sat in the recliner. Corrine sat on the floor between his legs. Kirk was on the couch across from them beside Julie, while Wyatt stood, leaning against the wall.

"Oh, stop," Corrine said. "I wouldn't expect you Neanderthals to understand anyway."

"I like it," Kirk said. "It brings the focal point to the back wall, where you could hang some art or nice family pictures."

"See?" Corrine said. "You guys could take some notes on class and decorating from Kirk."

"Oh, no," Kirk said. "My home is not winning any interior decorating awards."

Julie's ears perked up at the music that quietly played from a Bluetooth speaker in the corner of the room.

"Oh, man. Turn that up!" she said.

"Yes! I love this song," Corrine said. She grabbed her phone from the waistband of her leggings and almost dropped it from excitement. As she caught it and looked around the room with her eyes wide, Julie laughed and imitated applause. She bowed and then tapped the side buttons of the phone, raising the volume. Journey's "Separate Ways" blared out for everyone around.

"Oh my god. His voice is just the best," Julie said.

Phillip laughed. "You know this song is about him shacking up with a married woman, right?"

Corrine and Julie stopped swooning and scoffed in unison.

"Oh, stop. No, it's not." Corrine threw a pretzel at him.

A devious smile climbed across Phillip's face. "For real," he said. "Some chick he brought backstage. You ever listen to the lyrics? He basically says, 'Hey, I know we're going separate ways after this and you're gonna go back to your man. But I'll remember fucking you.'" Phillip winced and looked at Kirk. "Oooh, sorry. Uhh . . . courting? Embracing? I don't . . . I don't know an approved verbiage."

Kirk chuckled. "Oh, you don't have to do anything different on my account. In another life, I was in the Marines. I've heard it all."

Phillip turned his attention back to the girls. "Sorry to burst your bubble. Hopefully it didn't sully your Steve Perry love."

"Oh, stop," Wyatt said. "It's about divorce, you damn instigator."

Phillip narrowed his eyebrows. "Well, you're no fun."

Kirk slapped his knees with the palms of his hands. "Phillip, Corrine, thanks for having me over. But I do have to get going,"

"Oh, I'm sorry. We can turn the music down," Corrine said.

"Oh, it's nothing to do with that. I assure you. Gotta prepare for tomorrow's class." He grunted as he rocked forward and stood up. "I suppose I still can't convince you lot to join us for service tomorrow? Pastor Bettany is especially excited about the sermon."

"I don't think so, Kirk. Thanks for the offer."

"Well, I did try at least," he said, shaking his head. "Can't fault me for that."

"Not at all." Phillip threw his hands up and shrugged. "Maybe you'll wear us down. You never know!"

Adam and Connor emerged from Connor's room, both double-fisting empty soda cans.

"Mom, can I have some more pop?" Adam asked.

"Have some water, instead. You can't drink just pop all night."

His shoulders sank. "Okay," he said as he shuffled into the kitchen.

Kirk buttoned three of the middle buttons of his coat and draped his scarf around his neck. "Have a nice rest of your evening. Don't do anything that'll cost your security deposit," he said with a chuckle.

"See ya, Kirk," Corrine said as he walked out.

Phillip swung his leg over Corrine's head and stood up from the chair. "I'm gonna go get another drink. Anyone want anything?"

"No, babe," Corrine said. "I gotta take off soon. I shouldn't have anymore."

"You're working tonight?" Julie asked.

"Yeah, I'll be home about two. It shouldn't be too bad."

"I thought Adam was staying," Connor said, running in from the kitchen.

Corrine put her hands up defensively. "Relax. Yeah. Your dad will be here."

"You guys have to be quiet though. I work early," Phillip said.

"Okay," the boys said in tandem.

"Oh, man. Watching the boys all by yourself? You're brave," Wyatt said.

"It'll be fine. They'll just hang out while I catch some sleep before work."

"What time you gotta leave?" Wyatt asked.

"Early, and I got quite the drive. I got the call this morning. A school out in the city needs a well pump replaced for Monday. But, hey! Sunday is big money, so it's worth it."

"I guess," Wyatt said. "But we actually gotta get going too. The movie starts at seven."

"Oh, shoot. Okay. Adam, I love you. Be good," Julie said, kissing him on top of the head. "You guys know to call if you need anything."

"We'll be fine," Corrine said. "Besides, I'm leaving. They're Phillip's problem."

***

It wasn't long after everyone left, that the boys retreated to Connor's bedroom. Adam knew if he stuck to his plan, he'd be just fine. Keep himself distracted all night. He'd done it before. With Connor being an unknowing accomplice, they had plenty of entertainment and snacks to last until sun up. Or at least until their bodies tapped out without them realizing.

Phillip knocked on the door, grabbing their attention. "Hey, guys," he said. "I'm gonna shower and head to bed. Doors are locked. Let me know if you need anything, but only if it's an emergency. I don't need to know if we're out of Lucky Charms or whatever. Otherwise, make sure to keep it down, please."

"Okay, Dad," Connor said. "Good night."

"Good night, Mr. O'Leary."

For hours, they bounced from game to game. They started with Call of Duty, before moving to Grand Theft Auto, and then Fortnite. Adam aimed down the sight of the sniper rifle. Moments before he pulled the trigger, he was blindsided by someone, killing him instantly.

"Dammit!" Adam yelled on instinct.

"Shhh," Connor said. "My dad is sleeping."

"I know. I know. I'm sorry."

"Hey!" Phillip's voice boomed through the ceiling above them. "I said be quiet!"

"Sorry!" Connor said. He paused a moment before adding, "It was Adam!"

Adam smacked Connor in the shoulder.

Connor laughed and rubbed his arm. "Ow!"

"Stop. It's not funny. Your dad kinda scares me. I don't want him mad at me."

"Nah. He's cool. He's got a temper, but he's fine. He's probably already back asleep. Anyway, I'm hungry. Let's go see what's in the kitchen," Connor said. He hopped off the bed and walked toward the door.

Adam, still fixated on the game, looked at Connor, then back at the TV, then back to the door, where Connor had since vanished into the hallway.

"Hey, wait for me," he said in a high whisper. He lowered his head and walked straight down the dark hallway toward the beacon of light in the kitchen—toward the snacks and Connor.

"Don't leave me alone. Your house gives me the creeps."

"Oh, sweet. BBQ chips," Connor said. "And do we want the Chips Ahoy or the Oreos?"

"Uh, Oreos."

"Catch," Connor said. He tossed the chips to Adam and hopped off the counter with the cookies in his hands.

"Didn't you hear me? That first night I stayed—"

"I try not to think about it. But my mom thinks it's the girl."

"Wait, what? What girl?"

"A little girl died here. I heard her—"

Adam's jaw dropped. "The dead girl?"

"No, dude. My mom. She was talking about it one day. But she didn't tell me." He opened the refrigerator and grabbed two cans of Dr Pepper. "She thinks I don't know about it. But

I heard her say she can still feel her here."

"What are you talking about?"

"It was years ago. It happened in that hallway, I guess."

Adam's arms and neck grew goosebumps. He tried to speak, but his throat fell dry and closed in on him. After initially choking, he got out the words.

"You have a dead girl in the house?"

Connor shrugged. "I don't know. I haven't seen anything. My mom is kinda weird about that stuff." He turned and walked away, turning off the kitchen light on the way out.

"Dude, c'mon," Adam said, almost running into Connor as he caught up to him in the hallway.

<u>CHAPTER EIGHT</u>

Wyatt's grip on his marriage felt as hopeless as ever. He sat beside Julie, waiting for the movie to start, unsure of the right words to say. Or how to repair it. It was becoming increasingly evident, though, that he was foolish to think weekly counseling sessions and monthly scheduled date nights accomplished anything other than driving the wedge deeper and deeper.

The movie acted as a Band-Aid, as they were together and alone, though still not engaged with each other. Afterward, the walk back to the car snapped to the familiar feeling, cold and dark and awkward.

"I'm going to check on the boys," Julie said. She had her phone out and the speakerphone ringing before Wyatt could acknowledge what she'd said. Stephen's call unsurprisingly went to voicemail. She then called Adam, who answered.

"Hey Mom," Adam said over the speaker.

"Hey, bud. We just got out of the movie. Heading to get some food. Just wanted to make sure you were good."

It annoyed Wyatt how quickly her voice turned warm and endearing when talking to anyone other than him.

"Yeah, I'm good," Adam said. "We're just hanging out."

"Okay. If you need anything, we'll have our phones. Have

fun. I love you."

"Sounds good. Bye. Love you too," he said, and the call disconnected.

"I guess he's all good," Julie said to Wyatt.

Wyatt shrugged. "See? Nothing to worry about."

At the restaurant, Wyatt looked over the menu, then at his phone, then back to the menu. "What are you getting?" he asked.

Julie stared at her wine glass, slowly swirling around the contents. The pour, already half-finished, clung to the sides before running back down and joining the hypnotic whirlpool. "I don't even know. Maybe the steak and shrimp?"

Beads of condensation collected on the brass mug of his Moscow Mule, breaking free and running over Wyatt's fingers as he picked it up and took a sip. He couldn't help but watch Julie as she tried to distract herself. She stared off, and he followed her gaze to see what had her attention. A young couple at a nearby table shared a brownie topped with a scoop of vanilla ice cream. He swallowed hard and took a deep breath. "We don't have to do this anymore if you don't want to," he said. The words rang in his head much louder than the way he softly delivered them.

"What even is it that we're doing?" she asked.

"I'm trying to do what's right. Trying to keep our family together. I think. But if you truly want a separation—"

"Wyatt, again, I didn't say I wanted one. I said I don't see a future where we're both happy together. I just . . . I don't want to be one of those couples who stay together solely for their kids, only to resent each other when it's all said and done."

"Is that what's happening? You're starting to resent me?

"I don't know. I mean, no. I think I'm just . . ." She let out a disgusted sigh. "I don't want to hold each other back just because we're comfortable. People grow apart. It happens all the time."

"Julie," Wyatt said, "I love you. I really do. And I haven't pressed it lately, but for a while I've known. Of course I have. Known you weren't happy. I know you wanted more. And I tried to offer solutions. Until . . . until I just stopped, I guess. Because I can't be the only one, Jules. You always have this look like you want to be somewhere . . . anywhere else. I don't know the line between fighting for what I love versus making you feel trapped. But all I want is for you to be happy. Even—even if it's not with me. So, what it is you want? Truly. Is this even about us, or is it something deeper? Do you want to keep trying?"

The silence lingered only for a moment, but it was so thick and dark, it felt time had stopped. Wyatt floated in suspended animation like an acrobat who'd just let go of the trapeze in blind faith that someone would be there to catch him.

"I do," she said. "I really do. That's all I want. To be happy again. Together. But I feel like we're not even husband and wife, ya know? We're just comanaging a household. And—" She paused, tearing up. "And my boys are growing up and they don't need me anymore. No one needs me. Ever since I haven't been working, I'm just home. I do and do. No one cares. I don't expect a thank-you. But, just to feel wanted."

"I want you," Wyatt said. "I need you."

"You don't even look at me, Wyatt. Not really. When you do, it's with disdain. But when you feel me pulling away more, you act like it's all in my head," Julie said.

"I don't mean to. I just don't know how to talk to you anymore. Everything I say feels like it turns into an argument. So, I think I just . . . don't say anything. Like that's supposed to make it better or something. I don't know. I'm sorry." He reached across for her hand.

She sniffed in a tear that had rolled into the corner of her nose. "I know. I'm sorry too. And you're right. It's not just us. It's everything. I feel like I'm failing everything."

"Can we go somewhere else after this?" Wyatt suggested.

"Stay out? Maybe get some drinks or something?"

"Yeah. I'd like that," Julie said.

After they finished dinner, they walked to a nearby bar. Between the food and drinks and raw honesty, Wyatt didn't want the night to end. He was scared to push the issue, but it seemed like she felt the same. Really, he hoped this was a stepping stone, and not another false promise before falling back into the same routine tomorrow.

"Oh my god, it's after midnight," Julie said, glancing at her phone.

"Oh, damn. I didn't think we had it in us anymore," Wyatt said with a chuckle. "Want me to call an Uber?"

"Yeah, we probably should. I'm gonna text Corrine and see if she's home yet."

They cashed out their tab and waited for their ride at the bar.

"Oh, hold on. Corrine is calling me," Julie said. "Hey. Hey, hold on, I can't hear you." she said, and switched to speakerphone.

"Girl, your text was a mess. What the hell were you saying?" Corrine said.

"Oh, I was just seeing—" She looked around and talked louder over the noise. "Just seeing if you were home yet."

"Hold on. Are you guys still out? Holy shit, are you drunk? Good for you!"

"Oh, stop. But yeah," she said. "It—it's been a good night, actually. I'll talk to you more tomorrow about it. I just wanted to see if you were home yet and check on the kids."

"Yeah, I'm almost home. I'm sure they're passed out by now."

CHAPTER NINE

Adam and Connor ate their mountain of late-night snacks in Connor's room as they watched *The Last Airbender* on Netflix. The room light was off, but the glow of the television paired with the LEDs on Connor's computer in the corner provided plenty. While Adam sat alert and focused on the TV, Connor began nodding off. His head bounced as he fought off sleep, and Adam elbowed him in the arm.

"Hey," he said. "You're falling asleep."

"No, I'm not," Connor said.

This back-and-forth happened another two or three times until Adam gave up. He remained statuesque and forward-facing at the foot of Connor's bed, watching the screen. Connor's door creaked a slow but high-pitched cry, and Adam felt his heart thumping out of his chest. He didn't dare turn around.

"Hey guys." It was a soothing voice, one he immediately recognized. Adam exhaled and turned to face it.

"Hi, Corrine."

"Oh, jeez. Connor fell asleep on ya, huh?"

"Yeah."

"I'll be in the kitchen for a bit still. But you need anything before I head upstairs?"

"No. I'm good," he said. His jaw and shoulders were tense from sitting still for so long.

"You should get some sleep, too. Your mom will kill me if you're sleeping all day tomorrow."

"Okay. I will."

She closed the door behind her, and Adam was again all alone save for a sleeping friend and the ambient glow from the late-night screen. He crawled into his sleeping bag and stared at the ceiling, listening to Corrine move about the kitchen.

The more he tried to zone out, the more he grew hyperaware of every noise emanating from the house. Every gust of wind outside the window. Every pop of the house settling. He rolled onto his stomach for a bit, then onto his side away from the door. Unable to get comfortable, all he wanted was to be home. In his own room. In his own bed.

He'd tried. He'd really tried. But he was a coward, and he knew it. Not only did he not want to stay, but he hated himself for not wanting to stay. Hopefully, Stephen wouldn't find out. Somehow. Connor would tell him though, of course. It wasn't fair. Why did he always get this way? He had attempted to be brave. To stop being a baby, like his brother told him. But he'd failed. Defeated and embarrassed, he pulled out his phone and called his parents.

CHAPTER TEN

Julie took a deep exhale from the back seat of the Uber, wondering if her legs would operate to get inside. Wyatt thanked the driver, and she slid over to exit behind him. As she staggered up the moonlit sidewalk ahead of her husband, he called out to her, and she froze.

"What's wrong?" she said. Julie felt her jacket pockets, thinking she dropped something or left it in the ride.

"You look beautiful is all."

She smiled and pushed her hair behind her ear.

"You're drunk," she said.

"That's beside the point."

She slowly spun back around and continued up the sidewalk, swaying as she walked.

"Are you trying to seduce me?" Wyatt said.

"Is it working?"

They stumbled inside the house and straight to the bedroom. Wyatt kissed her neck as she slipped off her heels and then his belt. He picked her up and tossed her onto the bed. As Julie shimmied off her dress, Wyatt ran his mouth down the front of her. He stopped at her belly button and looked up. He smirked as she pushed his head back down. Almost immediately, a buzzing came from the nightstand.

"Oh?" he said without looking.

"Not that. It's my phone."

"Ignore it."

"It's Adam."

"Leave it. He probably wants to tell you about some video he watched," Wyatt said.

"At 2 a.m.?"

Julie ignored the call with one hand while she ran her fingers through her hair with the other, continuing to the back of her neck and down her chest. She wrapped her legs around Wyatt's head, and they got lost in each other again.

The phone rang once more.

Julie looked at it and deflated. She groaned in frustration as she slid back and sat up against the headboard.

"Okay, we actually should see what he wants," she said. Her demeanor changed on a dime from disappointment to an upbeat chirp as she answered the phone. "Hey, baby. What's up?"

"Mom, were you sleeping?"

"No, I'm still up," she said as she smiled and looked at Wyatt, who continued to kiss her thigh. "What's going on? You okay?"

"Can I come home? I can't sleep here. I really tried but I can't, Mom. I'm sorry."

"Baby, it will be okay. You're fine. It's just some jitters. Is Corrine still awake?"

"Yeah. I just heard her in the kitchen."

Julie covered the mouthpiece with her hand and mouthed to Wyatt, *He wants to come home.*

Wyatt plucked the phone from Julie's grip and twisted to face away from her.

"Hey, bud. . . No, I think you should stay. . . You'll thank me in the morning. . . Are you hurt, or did something happen? . . . Well, do you not feel safe with Corrine and Phillip? . . . What have you eaten since your mom and I left? . . . See, that's your problem. You know you shouldn't have sugar like that so late. It keeps you up. Close your eyes, take some deep breaths, and slowly count to fifty. I'm sure you'll sleep in no time. I love you. Here's your mom."

He tossed the phone back over to Julie. While it floated through the air, Julie could hear, "Wait, Dad" coming through the earpiece before the phone landed on the bed. She let it sit in front of her briefly, until she heard her son say, "Hello?" She picked it back up.

"Hey, baby. It's Mom again."

"Mom, please," Adam said, his voice practically begging.

She looked up at Wyatt, who vehemently shook his head no. Julie paused and sighed.

"Your dad is right. We'll see you in the morning. I love you. Get some sleep."

CHAPTER ELEVEN

The next morning, the silent house was a godsend to Julie's hangover. Wyatt had already left while she was still in bed, but at least he'd made coffee. She poured herself some from the half-full pot and sat on the couch to sip it.

She texted out, *Good Morning. I love you*, to the family group chat. She knew they would read it, but also didn't await a reply. She seldom got one. *Adam, I'll be there between eleven and noon. Be ready*, she added.

Julie readied herself for the day, took some ibuprofen, and headed out.

When Corrine answered the door to let Julie in, she was wiping the sleep from her eyes and holding a cup of coffee of her own.

"Good morning," she said.

"Hey," Julie said, much more chipper than her friend, despite still nursing the night before.

"Want some? I just made it. I just got up, actually."

"It's eleven o'clock."

"Yeah, I know. That Ambien sleep, though." She kissed her fingers and exploded them into the air. "Perfection."

"Oh, god."

"Yeah, when I finally was able to climb into bed I was out,

though. The wine helped."

Julie smiled and shook her head. "Anyway, I can't hang out. Sorry. We gotta get going. We've got some errands to run."

"Wait, wait. Tell me about last night."

"Oh, yeah," Julie said, having almost forgotten. "It was good. We talked. We had, like, an honest conversation about what we wanted. We're taking it slow. But it was . . . helpful."

"And then you guys . . ." Corrine finished her sentence by rubbing herself all over.

"Oh, stop," Julie said, laughing. "You're stupid." She looked around the corner to make sure the kids weren't listening in. *Three times*, she mouthed, holding up corresponding fingers.

"Attagirl!" Corrine said.

They walked down the hall and knocked on the door to Connor's room. After a second, Corrine pushed it open.

"Hey, where's Adam? He in the bathroom? His mom's here," she said.

Connor gave them a puzzled look. "He was gone when I got up. I just thought he got picked up super early."

"No, I told him I'd get him a bit before noon," Julie said. She looked around and noticed his backpack still sitting by the wall. "His bag is right there."

Connor smiled and shrugged. "I figured he forgot it." He jammed down the circle button and slid out of the storm, exhaling a small sigh of relief as he looked up at them. "He's always leaving stuff."

Corrine stood in front of him, blocking his view of the game. "Mom, move," he said, bobbing back and forth in an attempt to see around her.

"C'mon, Connor. Stop playing," Corrine said. "Where's Adam? It's not funny. They have stuff to do. Let's go."

"He's not here. Or if he is, he's playing hide and seek and I don't know it. I haven't seen him all morning."

"Jesus Christ. Adam!" Julie called back out into the hallway. "Come on. Get your shit! We gotta go!"

Nothing. Only silence.

She pulled out her phone and called her son, looking impatiently around the room, waiting for it to go off. Instead, the ringing came from the living room. Julie grabbed his bag and marched down the hall to locate the sound.

"Alright, fun's over. But you can't trick me, kiddo. So let's —" She stopped as she realized it was coming from the couch cushions. Julie reached in and pulled out Adam's phone. The messages she'd sent earlier still showed on the lockscreen as unread.

"Adam?" Julie called out once more, this time not frustrated, more inquiring. She was starting to worry, and was once again met with silence. "God," she said. "I'll bet it was Wyatt. Wasting my goddamn time. I told him I could pick him up."

She called her husband, and as it rang, she impatiently stood with one arm tucked under the other.

"Hello?" Wyatt said.

"Wyatt."

"Yeah. What's up?"

"I told you I was going to come out here and pick up Adam, right? What the hell are you doing?"

"What?"

"I even texted the family about it when I got up," she said.

"What are you talking about?"

"What time did you even get here? It's a good thing I did swing by, too. You didn't even get all his stuff," she continued without acknowledging his response.

"Julie, what the fuck are you talking about? I don't have Adam. He's still at Phillip and Corrine's."

"What?" she asked, her voice cracking.

Julie hung up, and the following moments passed as a blur. Corrine said something to her as she put on her coat, but the words just came out as muffled white noise. The room began to spin around her. Corrine grabbed Julie by the arm and led her outside, leaving Connor to search the house.

Julie and Corrine walked the area and yelled Adam's name over and over. Before long, Connor jogged up to them, still slipping his arm into his coat sleeve.

"I'll head down to the corner store," he said. "I'll bet he went for snacks or something."

"Hours ago?" Julie asked. "You said he's been gone all morning."

"I don't know," Connor said. "Maybe he went down to the park. He said he was getting bored with the games last night."

"Would he have gone down to the river?" Corrine asked.

"Oh god. By himself?" Julie said. "He's smarter than that, I hope."

"I don't know. We'll check."

They hurried down to the water and began walking along the bank calling his name.

"Adam!"

"Adam, are you out here?"

Nothing.

***

The police arrived in two squad cars just a few minutes after being called. Though they did so without the commanding alert of sirens and flashing lights, them pulling up to the house at all attracted neighbors to emerge from their homes and watch from their front lawns.

Two younger officers exited from one car. A tall, portly, middle-aged man climbed out from the other and approached Julie and Corrine. His solemn face contrasted with his slow yet confident stride up the sidewalk.

"Afternoon, Corrine," he said. "And you must be the mother of the boy who's gone missing," he added, somewhere between a declaration and a question.

"Y-yes. He's my son. Adam," Julie said.

"Ma'am, I'm Sheriff Paul Mason with the Marshport Police Department. I'm sorry this is happening. And I'll apologize now, but my bedside manner is, admittedly, downright dismal. So, if I come off at all as insensitive, just know my mission is to get this child home. Right off the jump, I wanna assure you we already have some things in motion to find the boy. The home security logs when the front and back doors are opened and closed. Corrine, while it's not in your name yet, I hope you don't mind we're already working to obtain that information. Now, please tell me everything you can think of, and I'll need a detailed description of the boy."

Julie and Corrine filled him in on everything they knew. The police asked the standard questions. When had he been seen last? What was he wearing? Were they sure he hadn't gotten picked up by someone else?

"Have you talked to the other parent?" the sheriff asked. "Most times it's that or another family member. Just checking, as it's a lot of manpower to utilize just to find out he was picked up by anyone else."

At the suggestion, Julie held back the urge to assault an officer.

As the police swept the house once more, Corrine called Phillip, leaving Julie all alone in the front yard. She searched for any kind of assistance or guidance. Anything that could make sense of the situation she found herself in. As she pulled out her phone to call Wyatt again, Corrine startled her by walking up behind her, still sharply talking to her husband.

"Goddammit, Phillip. Just get home," she said, and hung up. She looked up at Julie. "Hey, babe. Phillip said Adam was lying on the couch when he left for work about three-thirty."

"The couch?"

"Sir, check this out," the female officer said, walking up to the sheriff. She handed him a printout. "We got the home security activity of the house all night."

The sheriff waved Julie and Corrine to look it over together.

"Does any of this stand out to you?" Sheriff Mason asked.

"Uhh . . . not really," Corrine said. She ran her index finger down the time-stamped list of doors opening and closing. "I got home . . . here. The door opening here would have been when Phillip left for work. Wait, yeah. Here. There's a couple door openings after Phillip left for work. Like twenty minutes after."

Julie's knees buckled. She sat on the ground to avoid falling.

"There's no sign of forced entry on any of the doors or windows," the sheriff said. "Does anyone you know have a key?"

"We just moved in. So, just me and my husband. Oh! And the landlord. Kirk. Kirk Jameson."

Sheriff Mason signaled over the two officers, and they nodded in acknowledgment.

"We'll head over there now," one said.

"I'm gonna give the playground a good second look over before it all gets displaced by kids running around after Sunday school," the sheriff said. "There were a couple little ones and their mother there a bit ago. Gonna see if they seen anything out of the way, or even that could have been your boy's."

Wyatt's truck tires screeched and skidded to a stop in front of the house. Sheriff Mason turned and lowered his sunglasses to better see who pulled up so chaotically. When Wyatt hopped out and sprinted up to Julie, the sheriff fixed them back in place and headed over to the playground. Wyatt instantly wrapped her in his arms.

"He was taken," Julie said. "Our baby was taken from us."

"We'll find him."

They sat on the porch, and Corrine handed Julie a glass of water. Connor trudged back up to the house, and as the adults looked up at him, he bit his lip and shook his head. Julie buried her head into her folded arms.

Sheriff Mason approached the families, scribbling something down in his small notebook. "I'm gonna run over and talk to some of the neighbors. I know the Wrights have cameras. See if I can get anything from that." His phone rang. "Excuse me," he said, and turned away to answer.

Phillip arrived shortly after. He still had his shoe covers on. The knees of his work pants were dirty and wet. He had removed his work shirt, wearing only the white T-shirt underneath. "Hey, what did we find out? I got here as soon as I could," he said.

"Someone broke in and grabbed Adam," Corrine said. "I swear I locked the door when I got in last night. Phillip, I was right there and didn't even notice. I didn't even wake up or hear them."

"What do you mean? How do you know that?" Phillip asked.

"Like, half an hour after you left," Corrine said. "It's on the report. It shows someone came in after you left."

Phillip covered his mouth before running his hand down and gently tugging on his beard. "Wait," he said. "No, I . . . I forgot my coffee. I had to come back and get it."

"What?" Julie said. Equal waves of relief and hopelessness crashed over her.

Sheriff Mason turned back around. "Hold on. Hewitt, why don't you guys just head back into the station when you're done," he said into the phone. "We'll touch base there and write up the report." He disconnected and slid the phone back into the case attached to his belt. "So, Phillip, you can account for these two events on the report?"

"Yeah," Phillip said. "I was on my way to the shop, and realized I left my coffee on the kitchen counter. I turned back around to grab it."

"Then we're back to square one," he said, acknowledging

any wind being ripped from the sail of the crowd. "And, just to confirm, when you left either the first or second time, the boy was not in the van with you?"

"No," Phillip scoffed.

"Okay, we will need you to come into the station and give a proper report," Sheriff Mason said. He looked around at them. "All of you, please. Mr. and Mrs. Newcommer, if you have any pictures on hand, please give them to us at the station so we can share. Ma'am," he said to Julie, "we will do everything in our power to bring your son home. You have my word."

CHAPTER TWELVE

Sheriff Paul Mason arrived back at the station shortly behind the Newcommers and O'Learys. When he noticed he somehow was the last to arrive, he stopped just outside the entrance. He wiped the sweat off his forehead with the back of his sleeve and pulled open the door.

The Marshport Sheriff's office quickly grew cramped with both families, the sheriff, one of the MPD officers, and the receptionist all piled inside. Much of the space was a single open room sectioned into a lobby, a kitchenette area, and a workstation with connecting desks for Officers Hewitt and Daniels. Artificial dracaena and ficus trees sat sporadically along the walls and in front of the window beside the front door. The walls, all painted a pale greenish-gray, were decorated with a map of the town, a framed American flag, and an empty four-by-six-foot corkboard. In the back corner, a tiny, seldomly used holding cell sat vacant with only a cot and a metal bench inside. Along the back wall were three doors leading to an interrogation room, Sheriff Mason's office, and a supply closet that also served as both the file room and the evidence locker.

"I apologize the accommodations aren't more comfortable," he said as he sucked in his belly as much as possible and squeezed between Corrine and Wyatt. "We will try to get these statements fairly quickly in order to get out there ASAP and bring him home." He turned to the receptionist. "Gladys, can you hand me a notebook from the drawer there?"

She slid it open and frowned. "Fresh out, Sheriff."

Sheriff Mason took a deep breath, and looked back at the rest. "Give me one sec."

He walked into the supply closet, closed the door behind him, and grabbed a fresh legal pad from the pack on the wire shelf. On the floor beside him were stacked cardboard boxes of old cases, most of them open and shut. He rested his head against the shelf and closed his eyes for a moment of silence.

The quaint, calm town left the officers closer to public spokespeople rather than hardened officers of the law. The everyone-knows-everyone gossipy aspect of Marshport also kept crime minimal, aside from minor squabbles and grievances from those with nothing else to do but complain.

He joined them back in the reception area and asked Corrine to follow him into his office. She handed Phillip her jacket and her cross-body messenger bag, rubbed Julie's arm, and followed him in.

Sheriff Mason motioned toward the wooden chair with its fake-leather padded seat that stood in front of his desk, and after she sat down, he plopped into his own wheeled swivel chair behind the desk.

"Corrine, what time did you get home last night? I understand you got off kinda late." Sheriff Mason said in an all-business manner.

"I got home from work around one," she said.

"And the boy was there at that time?"

"Adam. Yes, I checked on them when I got home. He was still awake. But yeah."

"And then what did you do?"

"Well, I tried to wind down so I could get some sleep. I

took a sleeping pill and scrolled on my phone in the kitchen for a little bit."

Mason scribbled notes down in his pad as she spoke.

"Do you often take pills to sleep?" he asked.

"Yes, I have a prescription."

"And your husband was still there?"

"Yes. He was still in bed when I got home."

Her answers slowly grew more monotone, cracking into signs of irritation. Mason could only assume it was from the line of questioning.

"Do you know what time your husband left?" he asked.

"It was somewhere around three-thirty or so."

"Three thirty on a Sunday morning? Isn't that a little odd?"

"He doesn't always work weekends, but it was a special project. An emergency. Good money."

"And you didn't realize that the child wasn't in the house the next morning?"

Corrine put her head into her hands and sighed deeply.

"Look, I know how it sounds. But I didn't get up until around almost ten-thirty," she said.

"And what time did you realize the boy was missing?" Mason asked.

"Umm . . . when Julie got to my house close to eleven."

The officer opened his mouth to ask a follow-up, but Corrine cut him off.

"I thought they were in Connor's room playing games," she said.

"Where is your son now? He's just fine?"

"Yes. He's still at the house."

Mason put his pen and pad down and pinched his eyes with his thumb and middle finger.

"So let me get this straight," he said. "Your son's friend goes missing from your house in the middle of the night, and while we're here, you left your own son alone at that very house. Do you not find that strange?"

"I . . . I guess," Corrine said. Her facial expression flipped from concern to surprise. "Wait, do you think I had something to do with it? I'm the one who called you, Sheriff."

"No no. We're just gathering information. Trying to determine a timeline and narrow down the possibilities." He hesitated, and his burly eyebrows furrowed. "But the fact is, you were the last one to see the boy."

"Adam," she said.

"Right. You and your son were the last people to see him. We will actually need to talk to him too."

"Why?"

"Well by your accounts, he was sleeping right next to—"

"What do you mean by my accounts?"

"Well, Mrs. O'Leary, my officers did notice an empty wine bottle in their search. Either the kids drank it at the sleepover, or you failed to mention that you were mixing alcohol with the sleeping pills while taking care of children."

Corrine placed her hands on the edge of the desk and pushed off it slightly.

"Now hold on," she said. "They're old enough not to be watched like a hawk. And it was the middle of the night. I had to get some sleep. It's not like I was preparing for a parent-teacher conference."

The sheriff let her comment marinate as he tapped his pen against the desk.

"That's an odd argument when one of them went missing last night. Don't you think? My officers are going to do another sweep of the house. Is there anything we're going to find?"

"No. Nothing. We kept Adam, even though Phillip and I both had to work, so Julie and Wyatt could go out and spend some time together. They needed it."

"Needed it? Is there trouble at home?"

"Not really. I don't think they're fighting in front of the kids, or anything."

The sheriff scribbled that down in his pad.

"You think he would have run away?" Sheriff Mason asked.

"No! Well . . . no. I don't think so."

Sheriff Mason tapped his pen on the desk as he ventured down a train of thought away from the questioning. After a few seconds, he smacked his tongue against his teeth and looked back at Corrine.

"Back to your husband. You saw him leave?" the sheriff said.

"I was still awake when he left. Yeah."

"The first time or the second time?"

"I guess just the first time. I didn't even hear him come home the second time."

"So, you can't be sure he left alone."

"He didn't take Adam."

"I'm not insinuating he did. But truthfully, there's no way to rule it out, at this time."

"I just know! Okay? I think we're done," Corrine said.

"Yes. We're done. I may have some more questions later on."

"Do I need a lawyer?" she asked.

"Do you think you need a lawyer?"

Corrine stood up, paused to look at the sheriff once more, then turned to walk away. He followed her into the lobby, where she rejoined the others. She gave Julie a tight hug and through tears said, "I'm so sorry. We'll find him."

"Mr. O'Leary, can you head back now?" Sheriff Mason asked.

Phillip squeezed Julie's arm and walked past the sheriff into his office. He shut the door behind him and sat at the desk.

"Look. Sheriff," Phillip said. "I'll, of course, help answer anything and do whatever is in my power. But I don't have much more information than what my wife already told you. I was at work since early this morning."

"Just walk me through the events of last night for you," the sheriff said. "From after everyone left your house."

"Oh, nothing much. The boys played games and watched TV while I got some sleep before going in to work."

"It was just you three in the house at the time?"

"Yeah."

"You're sure? Weren't you sleeping?"

"I was. But I'd know if someone else was there before I went to bed." Phillip shook his head in disbelief. "I already told you. Both the boys were there when I left for work."

"The first time or the second time?"

"I mean, I didn't double-check when I ran in for a second to grab my coffee, no. So, I guess I can technically only account for the first time."

"Can we check the work van?"

"For Adam?"

"For anything that may help bring the boy back home to his family."

"I guess. What's going on? Am I a suspect?"

Sheriff Mason slammed his hand down onto the desk. "Phillip, I just told your wife the same thing I'm telling you. I am trying to establish a timeline of events and confirm the whereabouts of everyone last night. This is standard." He picked the pen and pad back up and continued, more subdued. "Now, please answer the questions. But it is interesting that your wife asked the same thing."

Phillip shot up, and the chair slid backward behind him in a screech.

"Listen, the more you're looking this way for answers, the longer it's gonna be before we can bring Adam back home. Stop wasting your time and maybe look at Kirk. The fucking weirdo is the only other person with a key to my house. Or maybe talk to the people across the street. See if they saw anything. Someone has to have seen something. Are we done?"

The sheriff motioned to the door. Phillip grabbed his coat

from the chair without sliding it back and walked out.

As Phillip exited the office, Officer Hewitt returned to the station. She approached Sheriff Mason's desk and handed him a form.

"I stopped by and talked to Kirk," she said, keeping her voice between the two of them. "It all checks out, like you thought. Got an alibi. Said he and Gregory were together working on Sunday School plans until late. After Gregory left, Kirk didn't leave the house. Gregory confirmed it." They watched quietly as Phillip hugged his wife and attempted to console his friends. Hewitt asked Mason, "You think they did it?"

"Just trying to ask the right questions," the sheriff replied. "I want to get a community search going immediately." He looked at his watch. "Why don't you and Dwight head down to the church? The after-service luncheon should still be going on. Darlene Wright's nosy self was hanging out during all the commotion. So, I'm sure the whole town's freaking out already. I'd like to get ahead of it and put them to good use. It'll also get everyone together to ask around if anyone saw anything of note last night."

"Sounds good, sir," Officer Hewitt said.

"I'm gonna finish up here with the parents."

They joined the rest of the group in the reception area. Officer Hewitt grabbed her coat along with her partner and they left, excusing themselves as they split the grieving foursome on the way out.

***

Julie silently sat beside Wyatt in Sheriff Mason's office. The sheriff had only stepped out to grab her a glass of water, but since time had all but stopped, she fell in and out of the moment. She watched the standing fan in the corner oscillate, then was hugging Adam goodbye the night before. The mini fridge in the corner buzzed, shocking her back into the room briefly until she was back on the phone with him being asked to pick him up. "Mom, please," were the last words she heard her son say before she hung up the phone. The sheriff handed Julie a Styrofoam cup filled with water that was not quite cold, and she was pulled right back into the room.

"I can't begin to imagine what the two of you are going through," the sheriff said. "I'm going to ask some questions, and we're going to do everything we can to help bring your son home safe. Now, some of these may seem odd. But I have to ask them."

Julie and Wyatt both nodded.

"Please. Anything," Julie said.

"Tell me a bit about your son," he said.

"He's just a normal kid," Julie said. "He likes video games and sports and cartoons."

"He your only child?"

"Um, no. We have another son, Stephen. He's fifteen," Wyatt said.

Julie's mouth dropped, and she shot up from her sunken slouch to full attention in the chair. "Oh, God. Stephen. I—"

"I already called Ross's dad and told him what's going on," Wyatt told her as he rubbed her shoulder. "He was going to drop Stephen off, but I didn't want him to be alone, so we're going to get him later. They said not to worry about it."

"How is he at school?" Sheriff Mason asked. "He have a lot of friends? In a lot of extracurriculars?"

"He's happy. His grades are good. And he's so smart," Julie said.

"He . . . he kind of has a hard time fitting in," Wyatt said. "He struggles. I mean, his brother is older by about four years. His best friend lives half an hour away."

"Right." The sheriff flipped through his papers. "You guys aren't from here, are you?"

"Just outside of town. More into the city."

"How long have you known Corrine and Phillip O'Leary?"

"Phillip and Wyatt were friends from school. We've been friends a long time," Julie said.

"So, you trust your children with them?"

"Oh, of course," Wyatt said.

"How are things at home?"

They both stammered as they looked at each other, then back at the sheriff.

"Good," Julie said.

"I mean, as good as any other," Wyatt added.

"Corrine mentioned there may be some troubles between the two of you, making the house less than ideal for a young boy."

"She did?" Julie said.

"Not verbatim. But yes."

"Well, I mean, sure, we have our problems. But we don't fight in front of the kids or anything."

Sheriff Mason smirked. "That's also eerily close to what she said. Do you see it possible at all that Adam would run away?"

Julie leaned forward and gripped the arms of the wooden chair. The Styrofoam cup, still in her hand, crumpled between them.

"No! No, that's absurd. He was at their house, and someone stole him in the middle of the night," Julie said.

Sheriff Mason nodded. "Of course. Of course." His voice was slow and calm, contrasting with their panicked tone. "We just want to get to the truth. And Mrs. Newcommer, the truth is, no one entered or exited that home all night. Other than the husband leaving for work."

CHAPTER THIRTEEN

Within hours, dozens of volunteers had convened at the park, walking distance from the O'Leary home. It was a sense of community Julie appreciated but could by no means enjoy under the circumstances. As she watched more people straggling in to join, she repeatedly tugged on her husband's coat sleeve.

"Wyatt, look," she said. "Look at everyone here to help."

"This is amazing." He put his arm around Julie's shoulder and squeezed her.

A tall, boxy man approached them. He appeared to be in his early sixties, with a bounce in his step like he'd be the ideal athlete for pickleball or shuffleboard. He had no hair on top of his head, but the graying horseshoe around the sides and back led into a thick silver beard.

"Good afternoon. I wanted to come over and introduce myself. My name is Gregory Calhoun. Gregory. Not Greg." He chuckled to himself as he shook Wyatt's hand. "I always say Greg sounds like a juvenile delinquent you'd find loitering outside of an arcade."

"Hi, Gregory. Thank you so much for helping today," Wyatt said.

"Oh, I wouldn't have it any other way," Gregory said. Each

of his sentences were punctuated in a slight uptick. "I am the head of the Marshport Town Council, member of the Marshport Historical Society, and also treasurer of the church. So if there is anything at all you need, please come find me. I'm sorry we are meeting under these conditions."

"Thank you," Julie said.

"Things like this just don't normally happen in this town." Gregory shook his head. "I don't want you to think bad of the place. Our crime rate is actually one of the best in the state. I like to think it's due to the structure we have in place, and the close-knit people. I mean, you should see the support at the town meetings and, oh my, the way the pews get packed on Sunday." His eyes grew wide. "Oh, but I want to put any reservations to bed. Even though you aren't locals, we will be as diligent as we would be if it were any Marshport child out there."

Julie opened her mouth to attempt a response, but none came. Wyatt stammered for a bit before being saved.

"Gregory!" shouted a voice that was instantly recognizable and comforting to hear. "Leave these poor people alone," Corrine said as she approached the group.

"I was trying to be consoling. I'm sure it had crossed their mind—"

"You're not helping," Corrine said, raising her hand to stop him from finishing. "Why don't you go touch base with Sheriff Mason?" She gave Julie and Wyatt both a hug greater than seemed possible from her small frame. "How ya doin' honey?"

"Oh, I just want to get started," Julie said. "Why is everyone just standing around? We're wasting time."

"We'll find him," Corrine said. "Sheriff Mason is just getting everything in order."

"I'm gonna go see what's taking so long," Wyatt said.

Before he could move, the sheriff's megaphone squealed, causing Julie to wince and turn her head. The crowd began to close in a bit, and Julie pushed her way toward the front.

Sheriff Mason unfolded a grid map of the area and held it up for everyone to see, before laying it flat on the hood of his police cruiser. Two main regions were sectioned off. The riverbank, which ran behind the house, and the woods beside it.

"First off," his voice boomed through the megaphone. "I want to thank everyone for dropping what they had planned this afternoon and helping us here today. I knew this community would step up, and by God you all have. Okay people, if for some reason you're unaware, here is who we're looking for." He held up an eight-by-ten photograph of Adam from when school had started, just a couple months earlier. "We want groups on either side of the river looking for anything of interest. The rest of us will be starting at the base of the woods and walking through until we come up on the school on the other side. Mom, you will be with the woods group. Dad, you'll be with the river. If he's out there hurt or scared, I need one of you to be the first person he sees."

As the search members came together for their assignments, Julie finally took notice of the sheer number of people who'd showed up. She smiled for the first time since arriving at the O'Learys' this afternoon, which seemed like a lifetime ago.

Working her way through the trees after, overwhelmed by the call to action, she had hope. The crew walked side by side through the woods, screaming Adam's name over and over.

"Adam! It's your mom, honey," Julie yelled. "Are you out here? You're not in trouble at all, if that's what you think. We just want to bring you back home safe. Adam!"

Her voice echoed through the woods and bounced off the other members of the search party calling out to the boy. They walked side by side, slowly and meticulously. Corrine and Connor walked beside her.

The leaves had already changed colors and begun to fall, making the ground visibility spotty. The majority of the party shuffled their feet as they looked for footprints, markings, or any belongings that may have been dropped by Adam—or someone who had him.

***

Wyatt and Phillip walked in tandem along the riverbank, with Wyatt remaining mostly quiet. He tried to keep his mind on the task at hand, fighting off any vivid worst-case scenario thoughts attempting to worm their way into his head.

"He, he can swim, right?" Phillip said, presumably to try and cheer his friend up, pointless as it was.

"Yeah. He can swim," Wyatt said in a distracted droll. His focus remained fixed on the river. "Was there anything you needed to tell Julie and me about last night? Did something happen? Anything you can remember?"

"No, man. I have no words, and I won't rest until Adam is brought back home. But I just . . . Fuck, I don't know."

Wyatt felt someone else approaching, and he turned around, with Phillip mirroring the action. A middle-aged man shambled up to them. His boots were dirty, and his hooded sweatshirt had an MBC screen-printed decal that had peeled away some with wear.

"We're wasting our time. You know that, right?" he said to them.

The brash absurdity caught Wyatt completely off guard.

"Excuse me?" he said. "Wasting our time? My son is missing. He could be out here."

"Could, yes. But he's not. What? Use your head. Are we supposed to believe he took a stroll down to the river in the middle of the night? And what, got swept away in the current? Look at this thing. It's basically a big creek. Tell me, do you really think your son would be out here?" He gestured out toward the river. "Or there, for any reason?"

"Do you know something we don't?" Wyatt asked.

The man wrenched his neck and looked around before leaning in closer. "Aliens," he said in a low, hushed tone.

Wyatt flipped. "Are you fucking serious?"

Phillip put himself in between them in an attempt to deescalate. Wyatt straightened his jacket and took a couple steps back.

"God dammit, get out of here if you're not going to actually help us." Wyatt shook his head in disgust and began walking again, with Phillip following behind him.

The man jogged back up behind them. "Sorry. I meant no disrespect. For real, though. I am helping you. They hole up in the woods. It's the only house on that side of the street there. The woods group may have a better chance, but I doubt they'll find anything, either. Think about it. Everyone in this town is always so chipper. It's almost eerie. But we're here for a reason, and I'm praying I'll be proven wrong." He ventured off by himself, closer to the shoreline.

Wyatt took a few long strides to catch up to him. "Wait wait! Sorry. What's your name?"

"Randy," the man said. "And really, no worries."

"So you say all this, but you live here," Wyatt said.

"Well yeah, the people are great and the local restaurants are amazing," Randy said without hesitation. He cupped his hands and blew his warm breath into them. "The thing is, though, weird shit does happen. The town's already talking all about your poor boy. How the police don't have anything. This is their way of casting as wide a net as possible. But it's all for naught. And that poor girl from a few years ago? The family moved shortly after, and then everyone here just moved on like nothing happened. But it . . . I mean . . ." He looked around again, before turning back to Wyatt. "I'd heard she was holding on to the doorframe so hard that when they found her, all her fingers were broken and the nails ripped clean off from the skin. That's how she died. She finally lost grip and hit that closet so hard the whole thing collapsed on her. Like she was being sucked in or something."

"Randy, can you come help me with this?" called someone else from the search party. A woman gestured him over, short and portly with a bob haircut tucked under a knitted winter hat.

"Who's that?" Wyatt asked as Randy trotted away.

"Oh, that's Gloria," Phillip said. "Head of the Marshport Beautification Committee. There's no true HOA here, but that's essentially our version of one." He shook his head. "That way, they can tax it and have everyone pay, whether you own or rent or visit. Because, according to her, the whole town should pitch in since the whole town is enjoyed by the people."

"Her and Randy together?" Wyatt said.

"No," Phillip said with a scoff. "Nah, he works for the town. Cleaning up, painting, changing the seasonal signs and shit. So he kind of works for her, I guess." Phillip scrunched his face and cocked his head. "Come to think of it, I don't think I've ever seen her with anyone. Gloria basically walks around with a gavel in hand and an iron rod shoved up her ass. And Randy's, well, out there, you could say. Sorry about that, by the way. He kinda snuck up on us."

"Is that true, though? What he said?"

"About the fucking aliens?"

"No, Phillip. The girl."

"Oh," he said. He dragged the toe of his boot in the rocky riverbed, kicking a few stones with a flick. "I have no idea. It was before we moved here. And like he said, no one ever talks about it. I didn't even know until we were looking at the new house."

Wyatt sat on the cold ground and placed his head in his hands.

"This is all my fault," he said.

"Hey, hey, hey," Phillip said. "Don't say that." He placed his hand on Wyatt's back. "We'll find him. Don't pay any attention to Randy."

"He's right though, isn't he?" Wyatt said. "Where the hell did he go? He wouldn't have come down here." Wyatt perked up, looked at the groups walking the river, and shot up to his feet. "Hey, where's your landlord at? Was he here with us?"

"Kirk? I think I saw him. Maybe he's with the other group."

"He's the only one who could get into the house, right? How well do you know him?"

"How well does anyone know their landlord? I mean, he's been over a few times for cookouts and shit. He's been our landlord for a while now, going back to the last place. He's attentive to the property. Better to stay in good graces with the guy who charges you rent than be at war, ya know."

"Phil, if there's anything weird you can remember from leaving for work . . ."

"I know this isn't a reassuring answer. But I barely know what I'm doing when I leave that early in the morning. Let alone pay attention to my surroundings."

"But you leave your family alone in the middle of the night sometimes."

"I just never really worried about it." His eyes shot around nervously, as if he regretted the words jumping out of his mouth, but he couldn't stop talking. "I mean, until now."

"Hey, everyone come over here!" Gloria yelled.

They dropped their things and rushed over.

"What did you find?" Wyatt asked in desperation. "Move. Move," he said, pushing his way to the front of the growing crowd. He looked down in anticipated horror, expecting to find a sock, or Adam's hat. Or god forbid a tooth or fingernail.

"This is the third time this week I have found fast-food wrappers down here on the riverbank," Gloria said. "We have talked about this at the last town meeting. But we will not become a trash town. If your children want to get high and throw garbage all over the place, you will pay the fines."

"Garbage?" Wyatt screamed, practically in her face. "You

called us over here for fucking garbage?"

"Well, I'm sorry for multitasking. I didn't mean to get your hopes up. But some of us live in this town and care about this community. We aren't just leaving after the search."

He took another step forward, and Phillip pulled him back by the shoulders.

"Okay, we're going to continue looking," Phillip said. "Gloria, you're unbelievable."

Wyatt continued to stare at her as he walked away.

She looked to the other bystanders for support, but they left her muttering under their breath. Randy picked up the trash and threw it in a bag tied to his belt.

"Need I remind you all that I wanted trash cans placed along the riverbank, and was shot down," she said. "This misunderstanding would not have happened if there weren't people here who want to live in filth. Blame them!"

They searched for hours, starting at one end of the river and making their way down to where it emptied into the lake. Spirits drained as they reached the end, hoping the crew walking the woods had better success in their part of the search.

***

Julie and Corrine sat on the hood of the O'Learys' Jeep. Julie leaned her head onto Corrine's shoulder and scrolled through the camera roll of her phone, each photo of Adam serving as a jagged reminder of her missing son. It wasn't long before she was looking at first day of school pictures from earlier in the year. He still had a line of summer freckles from cheek to cheek, and the awkward half smile in the photo caused her to sob. She clutched the phone to her chest. It was as close as she could get to holding Adam.

When the other half of the search party returned to the park, Julie jumped down and sprinted to meet them. She looked around for Wyatt, but he was notably missing. Eventually they found Phillip.

"Where's Wyatt?" Julie asked.

Phillip looked around, confused. "He was just here with the rest of us."

"Did he say anything?"

"No. Well, he was asking about Kirk. Maybe he went to find him. Was Kirk part of your group?"

"I haven't seen him all day," Corrine said.

Sheriff Mason approached the three of them.

"What's the next step?" Julie asked. "We just regrouping? Swapping search areas to get fresh eyes?"

"Is someone grabbing food?" Phillip asked. Corrine hit him in the shoulder. "What?" he said. "I'm not saying to stop. But people need to eat."

"Actually, about that," Mason said, "we've unfortunately done about all we can today."

"No, we can't stop," Julie said. "What about Adam?"

"Now ma'am, I was overjoyed by the amount of people who sprang into action when we needed them. But folks are tired and cold, and it will be getting dark soon. That's the gamble we made to get a jump on the search today."

"No, don't 'ma'am' me! Gamble? It's my child, not a fucking poker hand. You need to get out there and help me find my son—because I'm not stopping until we do."

"Now, listen," the sheriff said. "We have been all over these woods as well as up and down the river. If there were anything out there, we'd have found it."

"If he's out here, he's tired and cold, too," Julie said. "Don't you care about that? We can't just give up."

"Sweetie, no one is giving up," Corrine said, reaching out to rub Julie's arm.

"Stop it!" she said, recoiling. "Just stop. With your 'ma'ams', and your 'sweeties'. You're not going to calm me down. It's not a time to relax. My son is gone." Her attention whipped over to Corrine. "He was supposed to be at your house, and *you* didn't even realize he wasn't there."

Corrine staggered backward. "Julie, I—"

"No!" Julie's eyes narrowed as they welled up, looking at her friend. "Where is my fucking son?"

CHAPTER FOURTEEN

It was easier than Wyatt thought it would be to find Kirk's house. He spotted the man in front of the porch, trimming up bushes, or at least what was left of them after the leaves had fallen off, leaving just the bare branches. Wyatt slightly passed up the house, and the truck rocked forward after he hit the brake a bit too hard in the heat of the moment. He shifted into reverse, backed up a bit, and pulled forward into the driveway.

Kirk had already moved to picking up a few pieces of stray garbage from his yard, some fast-food napkins and a stray coffee cup. As he bent over, picking up the trash, he looked like he was trying to put a face to the vehicle in front of him. Glowing in the halogen running lights, he appeared like an animal frozen in the road, looking at oncoming traffic.

As Wyatt clenched the wheel and studied the man in front of him, he suddenly realized he didn't have a plan at all. It didn't matter. He killed the engine, popped the driver's door open with a metallic creak, and marched up to Kirk.

"Oh! Good evening, uhh, Wyatt, was it?" Kirk asked, standing up and removing his yard gloves.

Wyatt exhausted a disapproving chuckle and shook his head.

"Is it? I just left a search party for my missing son. So, I'm not doing so good."

"Ah, yes. I was going to check in with the sheriff. Did we find anything?"

"We? You weren't there, Kirk."

"Oh, I'm sorry about that. I would have been there of course. But I had to help at the church. Since much of the congregation joined the search today, we were short-handed cleaning up the luncheon. I would have been of little assistance out there anyway."

"Is that so? I find it odd that the guy who owns the house and is the only other one to have a key and knew the schedule of the tenants wasn't at the search for my son."

"Excuse me?"

"You fucking heard me," Wyatt said as he took a step forward. His phone began to vibrate, and he slipped it from his pocket to see Julie trying to get a hold of him.

"Wyatt, I know you're not a man of faith. But the Lord tests us in ways we cannot understand. We will find him."

He dismissed the call, but even after sliding the phone back into his pocket, he kept staring off in the same direction. He closed his eyes and took a deep, cleansing breath. This wasn't the Lord's work. Kirk was hiding something. He had to be. It was the only thing that made sense. Wyatt shot his eyes to the front door, then back to Kirk.

"I'm going to turn your house upside down until I find something."

"Son, I can't imagine the pain you're going through. So I'm going to ignore that accusation. You're just lashing out. But you're not going to tear my home apart because of it."

"Get out of my way," Wyatt said.

As he passed by, heading for the porch, Kirk grabbed him. Wyatt spun around and struck Kirk, and the man toppled to the ground.

"Where's Adam?" he said. He lifted Kirk by the hood of his

coat and punched him again. "Where is he? I know you know something. What are you hiding?"

"Help!" Kirk cried out.

"Hey, get off of him!" someone yelled. But neither Kirk nor Wyatt responded or acknowledged.

"What are you hiding?" Wyatt said as he attacked him. He gripped him by the shirt collar, then relentlessly and repeatedly hit him in the face, bloodying his lip and eye. "Tell me where he is!"

Wyatt stopped only after getting tackled by Gregory and some woman he didn't recognize.

"Mr. Newcommer, what in the world are you doing?" Gregory said, picking Wyatt up but still holding on to him and standing as a buffer between him and Kirk. "Kirk, are you okay? Angie, call the police."

Wyatt massaged his knuckles with his thumb. He looked back at the house. He could make it now, he knew it. But instead, he said, "He knows something. He has to."

The others looked to the injured man for some kind of response.

Kirk spit a mouthful of blood onto the ground and climbed back to his feet. His eye had already started to blacken. He pulled a handkerchief from his pocket and held it against his lower lip.

"Oh, my. Kirk, are you okay?" Gregory said.

"The police are on their way. I'm going to grab some ice," Angie said.

"I'm fine," said Kirk. "Thank you for getting here when you did."

"Well, I just pulled back up from the search and saw him attack you," Gregory said. "So, Kirk, I am a witness. I just wish I'd been here sooner. Oh, jeez. I was passing Frederick's Farm and saw the sign that he has his honey already, and I just had to stop and get some. Oh, if it weren't for my weakness for locally sourced, pure, jarred honey, I could have prevented this whole thing."

Surely this was all a dream, Wyatt thought.

The police car rolled up with the lights and siren blaring. Sheriff Mason approached the group, shouting,

"Mr. Newcommer, what in the hell is happening here?"

"Ask him," Wyatt snapped back. "He knows something. He has to."

"Mr. Newcommer, you're under arrest for assa—"

"No, no," Kirk said. "I'm okay. And he's hurting. Sheriff, I've already given my statement, and been questioned. But since Mr. Newcommer is here, we might as well talk openly. The reason they knew I had nothing to do with it is because I was with Gregory and Angie last night."

"All night?"

"Well, not all night, but we do our Bible study on Saturday and discuss what we want to go over with the youngsters in Sunday School the night before. We like to make sure that, no matter the age group, the weekly studies follow the same theme, and line up with Pastor Bettany's sermon at service. That way, everyone has the same sentiments heading out the door back home afterward. So, I left the O'Learys' and met with them. We snacked and discussed until, oh, it was close to eleven thirty."

"Yeah," said Wyatt, "I talked to my son at around one in the morning. So that timeline still works, you fucking creep."

The sheriff stepped toward him. "Mr. Newcommer, you need to settle yourself and stop slandering everyone in town."

"Mr. Newcommer," said Kirk, "may I remind you, my car needs a new muffler. You heard it a couple of times now and even mentioned it to me, yes? I have an appointment later this week with Marshport Motors. If I was leaving in the middle of the night, all the neighbors would surely hear me."

"Well, that's right," Gregory said. "I live right next door, and every time Kirk starts that thing up, I get a twitch in my left eye. Why, just yesterday I was making sure my winter decorations were all operational. You see, I separate Christmas decorations and winter decorations and put up the winter stuff early in the season but leave the Christmas ones until aft—"

"Gregory, what are you getting at?" the sheriff said.

"Well, when Kirk fired that thing up, I was so startled I dropped one of my illuminated snowflakes that hang on the front of the house and it shattered. So, I would know if he was leaving in the middle of the night."

Sheriff Mason shook his head and looked back at Kirk.

"Kirk, you sure you're good? It's really up to you. If you're okay and don't want to pursue charges . . ."

"Oh, no. I really cannot imagine what Mr. Newcommer is going through. And I understand how it looks."

"Wyatt, I think you should go. You've done enough here," the sheriff said.

"I'm telling you, if you don't look in his house now, I'll never find my son."

"Mr. Newcommer, Kirk has done you a solid favor after you have come onto his property, made wild and horrific accusations, and attacked him. If you don't go home, I will take you in for now disturbing the peace along with everything else."

"There's no fucking peace until I find what he did with my son!" Wyatt said as he stormed back to his truck.

He sat in the driver's seat in disbelief of how everything had just transpired. How was he the bad guy here? Sheriff Mason and Gregory had turned their attention to Kirk, checking his wounds. Angie rushed in with an ice pack, which Kirk waved off before walking back up his porch steps. As Wyatt pulled out and took off down the road, a spattering of other rubbernecks and bystanders emerged and whispered to one another. He watched them in the rear-view mirror until they disappeared from sight.

CHAPTER FIFTEEN

Julie thought back on Adam's life in hectic bursts of memories. How illusory the passing of time could be during a traumatic event. Not so much waves crashing into her one by one, but a storm at sea while she drifted aimlessly in the open waters, alone and malnourished.

She heard her own mother's voice in her head, telling her again how she'd be a terrible mother. Holding it over Julie's head whenever she needed help with anything. She thought about how when Stephen was fourteen months old, he had fallen off the couch and broken his arm. Her mother had berated her the entire way to the hospital, telling her she'd never be able to care for a child and yelling at her for putting her son's life in danger. She thought about how after Stephen, they weren't sure whether they wanted to have another child. And then, when they decided to, they had a hard time conceiving, even losing a child along the way.

Julie had never told Wyatt this, but she felt guilty the entire time they struggled to get pregnant again. Like it was her fault, and she was being punished by the universe for not being good enough. Not being present enough. Not being loving enough.

When people with too much audacity and no sense would

pry and ask if there was a reason for the boys' age gap, Julie and Wyatt would always make up some excuse. However, Adam was their miracle baby. Fertility clinics and consultations ate away at the nest egg they had accumulated, but it was all worth it in the end.

It seemed like not long ago he was just a baby, wobbly on all fours but refusing to crawl anywhere. He'd pick a destination and roll the entire way. It felt like just yesterday she'd sat at the table, helping him with his math homework because he struggled with dividing fractions. But at the same time, he'd been gone forever. The house was slightly colder. A bit darker. Eerily quieter. The feeling permeated the Newcommer home and lingered. Though merely a few days had passed since Adam went missing, the heavy feeling and thick, pungent air seemed like second nature. Like the memories of happier times were of a past life, and the stale emptiness was all that had ever existed.

Stephen walked in the front door after getting home from school. He hugged his mother.

"Hey, baby," she said, squeezing him back harder.

"Hey. You doing okay?" Stephen asked.

She held his face on either side and forced a smile.

"Yeah, I'm good. Just worried."

"I'm gonna go to my room. I have a lot of homework to do."

"Can . . . can you do it at the table?"

"Why?"

"Honestly? Because I can see you there."

"Mom, I'll be fine. I'll just be upstairs."

"Stephen," she said, without expanding on the thought.

He sighed. "Yeah."

***

Julie set the places at the table for dinner. She paused,

unsure whether to make a place for Adam or not. Neither choice felt right. Go with delusion, or the constant reminder that her baby boy was lost and going through who knows what? She set the plate down and sighed. Everything she did was meaningless. Every task not actively attempting to bring her son home was wasted energy. Why eat? Why sleep? Why make small talk with the neighbors, or go to the store, or check the mail? What was the point?

Wyatt approached her and kissed her forehead. It was welcome and warm, but she barely acknowledged it.

"I'm going to go get Stephen," he said as he squeezed her arm.

"He's just in the bathroom. He'll be down in a minute. He actually was doing his work at the table."

"Really? Wow."

"Yeah, I might have guilted him into it. But he went along."

Dinner was silent, except for the scraping of silverware on ceramic plates. Whatever conversations they normally engaged in felt trivial. They sat together around the round wooden table, but none of them were truly present. The only thing to talk about was what had happened, and none of them seemed to have the words or the answers.

Julie poked around at her green beans as she replayed the days leading up to the disappearance in her head on a loop. How he didn't want to stay. How she talked with Corrine, who basically blew the whole thing off. And then she let him stay anyway. What changed? Why did she allow it? The signs were there. The flags were there. Of something. Something not sitting right. Something waiting to happen. But she ignored them. Her child was scared. Scared of a place in the house where some other child was killed. That should have screamed danger. How horrible of a mother was she? She ignored her own instincts. She trusted someone else with the well-being of her child and the worst happened. And she knew! She knew they'd be in and out and not able to pay attention. He was only eleven. Sometimes she forgot just how young he was—something that came with him having a brother close to five years older. It was only natural.

"Julie, Stephen's trying to talk to you," Wyatt said.

"Huh? Oh, sorry. What's up?" she asked.

"I got a B on my history test," he said. "We're learning all about prohibition in Northern Ohio."

"Nice job, Stephen. That's great." Her words came out monotone and unconvincing, and she again lost herself in her uneaten plate of food.

"It is great," Wyatt said.

She looked up at him, and he stared back, furrowing his brow. He turned his attention back to Stephen.

"History was always the worst for me," he said. "I was always more of a science guy."

"Adam was too," Stephen said. "Remember when you guys watched Jurassic Park with him and he tried to catch all those mosquitoes, thinking he could do something with them?"

"Oh my god. He was so torn up with bites," Wyatt said, chuckling.

"Is . . ." Julie said, rejoining her family's plane of existence.

"What?" Wyatt and Stephen said in stereo.

"Adam is a science fan. Not was."

"It was an accident. I didn't mean . . . of course," Stephen said, choking on the words and realization.

"I can't do this. I can't just sit here," Julie said. "We're going to act like everything is normal and talk about our fucking day? No, I can't. Look, baby, I'm glad you did well on your test. I am. But also . . . who gives a shit? Who gives a shit? Who gives a shit about prohibition, or history, of fucking Jurassic Park? I can't just sit here and act like everything is fine. A piece of us is out there—and missing. And if we're here and warm and fed and joking, I mean, how fucking selfish? What kind of a mother lets her son get taken from her? And—and there's nothing. There's no sign of him anywhere." She continued in stuttered bursts between sobs. "I try so hard to be a good mom. I say I'd do anything for them, but I can't even keep them safe."

"Hey, hey, hey," Wyatt said. "Look, we will find him. We won't rest until he's home. You know that. The police are working to bring him back. He's out there."

"Out where? We searched and found nothing. Not even a hint. Not even a sliver of something. I haven't heard anything from any of those damned police since Sunday. Yeah, he's out there wondering why we haven't found him yet," she said.

"I know." Wyatt wrapped his hands around hers. "I know. But you need to eat. So, finish your food and we will call the sheriff. He said he'd touch base every day, and the fact he hasn't called us yet today is killing me."

"Can I be excused?" Stephen asked.

"Yeah. Take care of your plate," Wyatt said.

"I'm gonna be upstairs."

"No, take the living room. I want you down here with us," Wyatt said.

Stephen cleared his spot at the table and disappeared into the unlit living room. Before long, the glow of the television gave the area a dim luminescence.

***

Julie stood in the kitchen, still reeling, her mind still racing. It hadn't stopped since Adam had disappeared. She plucked Sheriff Mason's contact card off of the refrigerator and pinched it tighter with her thumb and forefinger as she dialed. Wyatt joined her, and she pressed the speaker icon and placed the phone on the counter. As it rang, the two hovered over it like it was the only thing giving them life. It rang four times, which felt like hundreds, until it clicked, and an elderly woman's voice came through the speaker.

"Marshport Sheriff's Office."

"Uh, yeah, hi," Julie said. She took a deep, cleansing breath for strength and continued. "This is Julie Newcommer. Um, Adam's mother. He's . . . he's missing. Sheriff Mason said to call whenever I needed. Well, I hadn't heard anything for almost a day and a half now, and I wondered if there was any information about him."

"Oh, yes. Good evening Mrs. Newcommer. I'll put you through to the sheriff."

"Tha—" Julie began, but the hold music cut her off.

"Mrs. Newcommer, good evening."

"Hi."

"Sounds like I'm on speaker. Is Mr. Newcommer also there?"

"Yeah." Wyatt nodded. "Yes, I'm here as well."

"What can I do for you folks tonight?"

"Well," he said, "it's been over a day since we last heard from you, and we're hoping you had some kind of news for us about Adam."

The sheriff loudly exhaled deeply yet sympathetically before answering.

"Unfortunately, not at this time," he said.

"Really? How?"

"Well, we do have some things we're following up with. But as for concrete information, or leads, I'm sorry to say there isn't much to go on, at this point in time."

"But . . . how is there nothing?"

"I didn't say there was nothing. Just nothing concrete just yet. There's a lot of moving pieces on an investigation like this. But you have my word, there's nothing I want more than to bring your son home safe. We are working diligently to find your boy, and I will touch base when I have information, of course."

"And until then?" Wyatt asked. He and Julie looked at each other in disbelief.

"And until then, day or night, feel free to give me a call.

Office calls are automatically forwarded to my cell after we take off from the office at the end of the day. So, you'll have full access to me."

"What do you mean at the end of the day?"

"Well, we serve as lawmen, but we aren't machines, Mr. Newcommer. We also sleep and eat and worship. But small a force as we are, we are dedicated to keeping the peace and upholding the Marshport standard of living. We will do everything in our power to find your son. You have yourselves a good night."

"I don't see that happening, Sheriff," Wyatt said.

"Well just know that you're in good hands here. And I know how to reach you, and you know how to reach me."

"Yup. We will," Julie said as she hung up the call.

She slid down the cabinets and melted into the kitchen floor. "I need to go lie down."

"You should go down there tomorrow," Wyatt said. "I don't feel like anything will happen if we don't. I need to go back to work, or I would."

She hadn't even realized he was going back to work. How could he? It didn't matter. If no one else would fight for Adam, she would.

"You're right. I will first thing after getting Stephen off to school. This is driving me crazy. I just want my baby back. I just— Oh, Wyatt. Where's our little boy?"

"We'll find him," he said. "We'll find him."

CHAPTER SIXTEEN

Julie sat in the drive-through of a McDonald's right off I-90. She didn't quite know what her next steps would be, but she knew she couldn't sit home and feel helpless any longer. Waiting. Waiting for a call that wouldn't come. Waiting for an update only to realize it was close to four in the evening and nothing had happened. Waiting and knowing, truth be told, that every second Adam was still missing, the chances of him being found slipped further and further away.

She sat in the breakfast traffic between the speaker box and the window and stared at the passenger seat. They didn't even look real. The stack of papers with Missing Child in big bold block letters at the top, and Adam's face center page directly below. The bottom provided contact information to both the Marshport police as well as her own number. She hated the thought of handing out fliers and asking random people if they've seen her son. But she hated sitting home and feeling helpless way more. The car behind her honked its horn, and she realized everyone in front of her had already grabbed their food and gone about their day.

Shortly after, she arrived at the Marshport community center. The bulletin board was filled with information about church bake sales and a Boy Scout fundraiser and a rummage sale this weekend on Oakdale. Someone was selling a car, and the Newtons had just had a litter of Labradoodle puppies.

Julie tightened her grip on the stack of missing child fliers she printed this morning. She looked around and saw some guy walking his dogs around the park. Two twenty-something women ran on the concrete track, which wrapped around the open lawn in the downtown square. Her throat swelled up when she spotted saw a mother and her young son, who couldn't have been more than two, kicking a soccer ball back and forth. His high-pitched belly laugh when she pretended to whiff her kick, and the ball rolled on past her.

Her heart beat heavier and heavier as the world began to close around her. A voice too upbeat and matter-of-fact snapped her back into the moment.

"Good morning, there, uh . . . Julie, was it?" Gregory said approaching her.

"Hi. Good morning."

"What do we have here?"

"Oh, I'm here to hand out and post fliers. I'm trying to find anyone who could have information on Adam."

"Oh, of course. Of course. I get that, and I want to help bring the boy home in any way we can. But, and well, this is a bit awkward. Anything that goes on this board must first be approved by the town council."

"What?"

"Yeah, it is clearly stated here in the top corner of the board." Gregory pointed to a laminated yellow sign in the upper right corner of the bulletin board. "Now, we are meeting Friday evening. We have a tight agenda, but I could squeeze it in and bring it up. We'd have to vote. But I feel surely—"

"It's my missing child! Not a fucking couch for sale."

"Yes. I get that. And I feel terrible. Believe me. But rules are rules, and if we start to bend them, who knows where we will end up. We can't just have this becoming a free-for-all. Now . . ." Gregory looked around, presumably to make sure no one was listening in, but no one else was nearby. He leaned in and continued with a more hushed tone. "We can get this expedited if you get approval straight from the sheriff's office. You have to fill out a form and get it signed by the sheriff, but that would get you on there today."

"Fuck your board. I'm just going to shove them down people's throats. I will find my son."

"Oooh, um, solicitation and panhandling are strictly against the Marshport bylaws. That one is actually a fine rather than just a removal from the bulletin board. That would be pretty counterproductive!" Gregory chuckled to himself. "Good thing I was here, eh?"

Julie stretched her neck and rolled her shoulders forward and backward. She looked up at the petty, self-congratulating man and had no words for him. She walked back to her car, got inside, and gripped the steering wheel. She screamed. She screamed so loud a few onlookers stopped what they were doing, but she paid them no mind. Afterward, she half expected Gregory and his puffy athletic vest to knock on her window and casually mention a noise ordinance violation.

She wouldn't give him the satisfaction, but she'd been planning on stopping at the sheriff's station next anyway to see if they'd found anything. Leads? Witnesses? Suspects? She'd have taken almost any breadcrumb or dull glimmer of light at this point. Even the fucking aliens guy Wyatt mentioned was starting to make her mind wander into what-if scenarios, which truly scared her.

As she entered the police station, she instantly saw red. One officer was talking on the phone to someone about what appeared to be a dispute about a fence installation location. The other stood beside a dirty microwave in the dinette area, warming up a cinnamon roll while the secretary worked a sudoku puzzle.

"Is Sheriff Mason in?" Julie asked, her tone sharp and to the point.

"Yeah, let me make sure he's available." Gladys rolled back in her chair a bit and looked into his office. "Hey Sheriff, you free?"

"Yeah, what's up?"

"Someone here to see you." She rolled back over to the desk. "What'd you say your name was again?"

Julie wrung the fliers of her missing son in her clenched fists.

"I'm Julie Newcommer. Mother of the missing child he's supposed to be looking for."

Before the secretary had a chance to respond, or blankly relay the information, the sheriff emerged from the back office.

"Mrs. Newcommer, I was expecting you, actually. Gregory told me you might stop by. I needed to talk to you anyway, so this works perfectly."

"What did you find?"

"Yeah," he said as he removed his hat and placed it on the desk. "I wanted to touch base with you. But just to explain we're still cold. Unfortunately. We are looking at all angles and pursuing all avenues."

"What do you mean, cold? Like you have nothing? How? My son has been missing for three days. He was in that house, and then he wasn't. There's no one in this godforsaken town that saw anything? Heard anything? Have you knocked down doors? Who have you questioned? What the hell have you actually done? Who's even in charge of finding Adam?"

"Now look, I understand your concern. I really do. And our whole town is absolutely shaken. They can't believe something like this happened right under our noses. We're looking over the timeline of the night, and trying to make sense of it. There's a lot of factors at play, and we're all prayin' on it in the meantime."

"Praying on it?" she said, almost in disbelief. "Prayers won't bring my son back home safely. Just actual fucking police work."

"Now listen, we are doing everything possible to get your son back. Believe me. There's more to police work than going around and screaming and bullying people for information. Now I understand and take no offense. But do not undermine my guys or my process."

"Process? You don't even have any leads."

"We do. But I also have to stop you there and say while I want for you to stay positive and informed, we're not going to run every decision and conversation by you. You just have to trust us."

Julie couldn't tell if he was attempting to calm or belittle her.

"Trust?" she said, as much to herself as to the sheriff. Julie's phone rang, and she looked down to see the school calling her. She slid her thumb down to ignore the call. "Until I have Adam back, I will not trust. I will not rest. And I damn sure will not sit idly by while my child is alone and scared and relying on me to do everything in my power to get him home."

Her phone rang again, the same number.

"What?" she said into it without breaking her gaze from the sheriff.

"Mrs. Newcommer? This is Principal Collins from Torwood High School. There has been an incident with Stephen, and we need you to come down."

"What? Is he okay?"

"He's all right. He was involved in a fight, and we need either you or his father to come."

"He what? He's never been in a fight before. Okay, um . . . yeah, one of us will be there as soon as we can."

She ended the call and immediately reached out to Wyatt, who didn't answer. She mouthed a string of obscenities to herself and slipped it back into her pocket.

"I need to go," she said.

Sheriff Mason nodded and gestured cordially toward the door. "One more thing, while I've got you here. I'm not sure if you're aware, because Kirk was afraid to say anything, but he had to go to the urgent care after that run-in with your husband the other day. Appears misplaced aggression may run in the family, now that I think about it. But he was more torn up than initially believed."

"I'll let Wyatt know."

"When you can get a hold of him, I suppose?"

Julie turned to walk away, but Sheriff Mason stopped her.

"Mrs. Newcommer," he said. He handed her a signed form with official Marshport header at the top. "Here's your approval to hang posters and hand out fliers. I had to add the note about the handouts to keep people from giving you a hard time. If anyone does, please let me know. These are extenuating circumstances, after all. And we will keep in steady contact with you. You have my word."

"Th-thank you," she said, grabbing the paper and walking out the door

CHAPTER SEVENTEEN

Julie slammed Stephen's bookbag onto the kitchen table. "Fighting? Stephen, what the hell?"

"I didn't even start it," he said. He pled his case hunched over and timid, though he normally stood three inches taller than his mother.

"You dislocated his shoulder!"

"Mom, I—"

"Hey, hey, hey," Wyatt chimed in as he walked in the front door and followed the noise of their conversation to the kitchen. "What's going on?"

"I've been trying to call you for hours," Julie said to Wyatt. "Your son got suspended from school for fighting. I mean really, Stephen, with everything else? I just . . .I can't handle this right now."

"Oh, now you care?" Stephen said. "I thought you'd be happy. I can't go to school, and now I just have to sit here and let you stare at me to make sure I don't disappear, too!"

Julie's jaw fell.

"Listen you ungrateful little— We're going to have to pay that boy's hospital bills. Oh, God. I have to call their pa—"

"Oh, fuck him," Stephen said, then added, mostly under his breath, "I should have broken his arm."

"Stephen Michael Newcommer, watch your mouth," Wyatt said, adding nothing to the actual discussion at hand.

"He said Adam was chopped up in a ditch somewhere!"

"What?" Julie said. Her face flashed ice-cold as she was hit with the intrusive visual.

Stephen let out a deep exhale. He rubbed his eyes and began speaking in a lower tone. "I was excused because when I took it the first time, I couldn't breathe and ran out of the class to the bathroom. I talked to Mr. Wilkins after, and he said to come back during study hall. When I left to go retake it, Brayden Samuels said I get whatever I want right now because my brother was chopped up in a ditch."

"Oh, sweetie," Julie said. "I'm so sorry. Why didn't you tell me?"

"I tried! You weren't even listening to me."

"I . . ." Julie searched for a response as she pulled her son closer. "I'm sorry. I'll call the school in the morning. Make sure they have the full story. It doesn't change what happened, but it might affect their decision about what to do about it."

She held him, and he held her even tighter. As Stephen began to shake against her with his face buried into her shoulder, she scratched the back of his head.

"It's my fault, Mom," Stephen said. "It's my fault he's gone."

Wyatt shook his head. "No, don't say that."

"That's not true," Julie added.

"It is. I told him he was scared of nothing. He wanted me to stay with him. I'm supposed to protect him."

"Oh, stop," Julie said. "What happened to Adam is not at all your fault. Please, please, please do not feel guilty about it."

"He wanted me there. Then he asked if he could come to Ross's with me, and I told him no." Stephen wiped the tears from his flushed cheeks and eyes, but they collected again immediately after. "I shoulda just let him come with me. If I did, he'd still . . . he wouldn't have . . ."

"Shh. Shh," Julie said, trying to calm him. "You have nothing to feel guilty about. Look at me." She grabbed his face and looked him in the eyes. "Do not carry this with you. It is not your fault. Let me hear you say it."

Stephen sobbed and attempted to catch his breath.

"Let me hear you say it," Julie said again.

"It's not—it's not my fault."

"Again."

"It's not my fault."

"Why don't you go up to your room and lie down for a bit," Wyatt said. "We'll let you know when dinner is done."

Stephen grabbed his bookbag and phone, and a soda from the fridge, then ran up the stairs.

Julie laid her head on the back of the couch and covered her face with her hands. Wyatt squeezed her thigh.

"What are we gonna do?" he asked.

Before she could answer, they both jumped from a knock at the front door.

"You expecting anyone?" Wyatt said.

"Not me."

"I can take care of dinner, if you want to grab the door."

"Yeah. That sounds great," Julie said.

Standing at the door were two police officers. Not from Marshport. Julie didn't recognize them, but their badges said Torwood Police Department. Her stomach flopped inside her, and a million scenarios ran through her mind at once. Her immediate realization was that Adam was not with them. But their demeanor, looking all business and without a bit of somberness to them, was oddly reassuring.

"Hello?" she said.

"Is Wyatt Newcommer home?"

"Yeah," she said, then hollered, "Uhh, Wyatt?"

Wyatt walked up the hall to the front door, drying his hands on the front of his jeans. "Hi. Can I help you?"

"Are you Wyatt Newcommer?"

"Yeah, that's me."

"This is for you," one said as he handed him a manila envelope.

"What is this?"

"Does this have anything to do with Adam?" Julie asked.

"I'm not sure, ma'am. We were just sent to deliver the notice."

"You all have a good night," one of the officers said. He tipped his cap as they turned and walked back to their car.

"What is it?" Julie asked as Wyatt read over the papers inside.

"It's a fucking restraining order from Kirk Jameson. It says I need to stay five hundred feet away from him at all times."

"Are you serious? Well, the sheriff did say he had to go to urgent care afterward. But he didn't say anything about charges being pressed against you." Her face changed from questioning to frustrated. "Oh god, Wyatt. You had to go and attack him, didn't you?"

"Really? This is bullshit and you know it. There's a declaration attached of a warrant for my arrest if I even come into town. How am I the bad guy here? Julie, what the fuck is happening?"

"I don't know. Look, I wanted to talk to you about this already, but this seals it. I don't trust them to find our son. They're too close to it, or lazy, or something. I don't even know. But we're getting nowhere."

"So, what are we supposed to do? I can't even do anything about it."

"There's people you can hire. Like, someone to focus on your specific case."

"You mean like a private investigator? People actually use those?"

"All the time. Honestly, I was already kind of looking into it earlier. There's online resources with ratings, reviews, you name it. I've still got some pulled up."

They looked through the profiles Julie had saved and called a few. Two, they couldn't get a hold of. Others were sympathetic to their situation but not currently available, or wanted far more money up front than the Newcommers could take on at the moment. Finally, they found someone who seemed very invested and agreed to meet with them the following day.

CHAPTER EIGHTEEN

For the first time that year, the temperature dipped low enough to frost everything overnight. The crystallized blades crunched under Wyatt and Julie's feet as they cut through the grass to the car. The entirety of the front yard glistened in the rising sun.

Wyatt handed the keys to Julie. "Can you heat the car up while I find the scraper?"

She slid into the passenger seat, and as Wyatt searched the rear hatch of the Escape, the engine turned and the vents roared at full blast. He found what he was looking for under a gray fleece throw blanket and an empty McDonald's bag.

After making a hole in the frosted windshield big enough to see into the car, he noticed Julie staring straight forward as she rocked back and forth, her hands tucked under her knees.

He leaned around and opened the driver's door, poking his head inside. "Julie?"

"Do you think . . . do you think he's out stuck in this?" she asked. "His shoes. His jacket. It was all still at Corrine's."

Wyatt sank and plopped the rest of the way into the car.

"I know. I don't—I don't have anything that will be reassuring. Except for empty promises. But that's why we're going to get some help."

Wyatt let the car do the rest of the work defrosting the windows. During the silent morning ride, his mind ran through the familiar looped cycle of thoughts and worries and fears. He glanced over at his wife, who stared off into space herself, probably busy torturing herself with the same.

***

The private investigator, Damon Williams, worked out of Cleveland but had agreed to meet with them at a diner halfway between them. Wyatt and Julie arrived early in an attempt to calm their nerves as well as make sure they were on the same page. They sat across from each other in a booth. Wyatt ordered a western omelet, home fries, and wheat toast. Julie simply sipped on some coffee.

Her phone buzzed as the waitress poured a refill into her cup.

"It's just your sister. She got Stephen, and wanted to make sure we knew." She sighed as she slid it back into her purse. "She's the best."

"Yeah. Yeah, she is," Wyatt blankly agreed as he stared at the diner's front glass door and chipped away at his omelet.

The hanging string of bells chimed as Damon walked in. Before the door closed behind him, someone behind the counter yelled, "Go ahead and sit anywhere, sweetie! We'll be right with ya'."

He looked around the diner, and Wyatt waved him over as Julie switched to the opposite side of the booth to sit next to her husband.

Conflicted as he was before, Wyatt suddenly felt uneasy about the meeting. He wasn't sure why, but he always imagined private investigators as something created for Hollywood. A mix between Keith Mars and Jake Gittes, wearing a long beige trench coat to add a whisper of mystery. Damon approached him appearing like he was plucked straight from passing as a high schooler in some Netflix show. Somewhere between eighteen and thirty-two, with a fitted Dickie's jacket and matching winter knit hat. Last night, Wyatt had assumed the profile photo provided was simply in need of updating, but somehow this guy looked even younger in person.

"Are you the Newcommers?" Damon asked.

"Yes," said Julie. "Hi."

"Hi, I'm Damon," he said. "Oh, man. It's cold this morning."

"I'm Julie. We spoke on the phone."

"Right. Nice to meet you."

"Thank you for driving out here."

"Well, it's the least I could do." Damon turned to Wyatt and extended his hand. "And you must be Mr. Newcommer."

"Yes. Please, call me Wyatt," he said.

Damon removed his jacket and beanie and tossed them into the corner of the booth. His blue flannel shirt was loosely tucked into black jeans. His dark hair and stubbly beard both looked freshly trimmed and styled.

"Did you bring a picture of Adam with you?" he asked as he sat down.

"Yeah," Wyatt said, and slid the picture across the table.

As Damon looked at the photo, he unbuttoned his wrist cuffs and rolled up his sleeves, exposing the tattooed forearms and smartwatch around his wrist.

"Have . . . how much experience do you have as a private investigator?" Wyatt asked.

"Almost ten years."

Wyatt wiped his mouth with a napkin in attempt to hide his surprise.

"Really? Wow," he said.

Julie snapped her head toward him. "Wyatt!"

So, he must not have been using a good poker face after all. Or she just knew him better.

"No, Jules. I know we need help, but c'mon. Do you really think this is the answer?"

She looked back at Damon, who pretended to somehow not hear to the two of them arguing.

"What my husband is trying to ask, is if you have any references. You do seem younger than we expected. No offense."

"No, no. I get that. I'm older than I look. Don't worry. Blessed with a childish demeanor, I suppose. But I've got sisters, ya know? They told me you gotta moisturize." Damon chuckled.

As Wyatt sat stone-faced, the kid's chuckle trailed off.

"Uhh . . . yes. References. I have references." He slid over a thin black folder.

Wyatt flipped the folder open and studied it as he continued the conversation.

"How'd you get into this?" Wyatt asked.

"My uncle has a practice. He was a police officer in Cleveland, but always felt the force was spread too thin and he couldn't really help people. Not the way he truly wanted to, ya know? I helped him around the office when I was younger and loved it. I got my license as soon as I could and never looked back."

"So, you work with your uncle?" Wyatt said. "That makes more sense."

"Well, we're a team," Damon said. "I'd be taking this on alone, though."

Wyatt and Julie looked at each other.

"I'm going to run to the bathroom real quick," Damon said. "It was a bit of a drive to get out here. If the waitress comes, can you please have her get me a coffee?" He slid out of the booth, scanned around the diner, and nodded toward the back corner. He tapped the tabletop twice, and said, "Excuse me. I'll be right back," before leaving the parents to discuss in privacy.

As he walked away, Wyatt turned to Julie.

"Are you kidding me?" he said. "He's like twelve. He just do this when taking a break from Fortnite?" Two older men in the booth beside them looked his way, so he must have been louder than intended.

"What choice do we have?" asked Julie. "The police are no help. They practically shut down when I show up. He'll help. I mean, look, if his references check out."

"Do we need him? Or are we just grasping at straws? Don't these guys normally rely on connections and relationships to talk to people? He'd be going in blind."

"Maybe that's what we need, Wyatt. Someone who's a stranger to find something there for us. I just . . . I need something. We need our baby back."

The two turned their attention back to the contents of the folder, though Wyatt was mostly looking for any reason to not hire him. From the corner of his eye, he saw Damon creeping back up to the table.

"Still no coffee, I see," Damon said. "Just a sec."

Wyatt was slightly impressed as he witnessed Damon grab a clean mug flipped upside down on the diner counter and pour himself a cup from the pot, looking back and forth as he did so. Either no one saw him, or no one cared, because nobody said a word. Damon sat back down and smiled, blowing the steam from the top and taking a sip.

"For what it's worth," Damon said, "I don't play Fortnite. I'm more of a Legend of Zelda guy, actually. I like the puzzles."

Wyatt stammered, "Oh, I didn't mean—"

Julie gave Wyatt a disgusted look. "I apologize for my husband."

"Don't worry about it. I understand. Really. You need to feel like you're in good hands. Mr. and Mrs. Newcommer, you can trust me."

"Look, Damon," Wyatt said. "Combing through your

references, I can't help but ask. Have you ever even done a case like this before?"

Damon took his hands off his coffee and slid his palms back and forth on the table.

"Not exactly of this scale. No. Not that I'm unprepared. It just hasn't been brought to me. I mean, thank God, obviously. Right? Mostly I've done insurance claim scams. Some adultery suspicions. Things of that sort. But please know, I would dive headfirst into this and am definitely the guy you're looking for."

Wyatt turned to Julie, who looked back at him with pleading eyes.

"I appreciate you coming all this way," Wyatt said. "But I think we may go in anothe—"

"Listen, I know you guys are hurting. And it's awkward to discuss this with me sitting right here. But here is my card. I'd say take the day and call me tomorrow, but time is obviously of the essence. Just know, I will stop at nothing to get you guys answers."

"I don't want answers!" Julie said, slamming her hand on the table. "I want my son back. I haven't slept. I'm not eating. Any downtime I get, I just think about Adam and what could have happened to him. How he must be so scared. And hurt."

"Of course," Damon said. "I will leave you alone. Let me know." He placed a five-dollar bill on the table. "This is for the coffee, if they actually charge me."

Wyatt glanced to Julie, who stared down at the table, looking like she'd just lost Adam all over again. He sighed and massaged his temples before turning his attention back to Damon.

"No. Please," Wyatt said. "Please help us."

"It would be my pleasure," Damon said. "Tell me everything you can about Adam and that night. Down to the smallest detail."

CHAPTER NINETEEN

Damon sat and bounced his leg up and down, waiting in the lobby of the Marshport Sheriff's Office. He assumed getting there at 8 a.m. would make it easy to talk with the sheriff first thing. But going on eight thirty, he was still waiting, and even largely ignored by the receptionist, except for being asked for a four-letter word for a pasta type. It was orzo.

The sheriff finally entered and immediately looked at the stranger seated inside the door. "Who's the kid?" he asked.

"Said he's here to see you," Gladys said. "What did you say your name was, again?"

"I didn't get a chance to before you told me to just wait, actually. My name is Damon Williams, and I'm a private investigator. Wyatt and Julie Newcommer hired me to help find their son, Adam."

"I'm sorry, honey, that's a lot. I kind of zoned out. Sheriff, you hear that?"

"Yeah. Thanks, Gladys. Go ahead and follow me, son."

Damon knocked his fist on the front desk and thanked Gladys before heading back to the sheriff's office. He extended a hand and introduced himself.

"Hi, Sheriff. Damon Williams. The Newcommers hired me to help find their son, Adam."

"Yep," the sheriff said as he looked through a stack of mail on his desk. "I heard the spiel out there. No offense, son. But what do they expect you to be able to do that we haven't been doing already since day one?"

Damon realized his hand was still extended, and slipped it into his pocket. "It's nothing that you aren't doing," he said. "Moreso, they believe, quite frankly, the department doesn't seem to have the resources to handle something like this. I just want you to know, I'm not trying to step on any toes. But just, if you see me around town, or hear about someone making the rounds, I wanted to introduce myself first. I feel like we should work together."

"Together, huh?" Sheriff Mason tapped his pen against the desk before putting it back into the holder in front of him. "You got anything to prove you are who you say you are? For all I know you're some internet leech tryin' to make a buck exploiting a hurting family."

"Of course," Damon said. As he lifted his jacket to reach his wallet, the holster attached to his belt attracted the sheriff's attention.

"Oh, you won't need that around here," the sheriff said, nodding toward the pistol as he reached for the card.

"I don't plan on it, but it's all on the up and up. I can show that too if needed."

"Nah. Not necessary." Sheriff Mason studied the license and then Damon. He handed it back. "You ever deal with a missing person case before? Or more specifically, a missing child? Ya see, in a case like this, there's much more to it than people think. You need to keep the family at ease as much as you're looking for the kid. Try to keep the parents optimistic, while at the same time not filling their heads with false promises. It's extremely delicate."

"Well, no. But I get it."

"You seem awfully young. How'd you get into this business, anyway?"

That was already getting old.

"Not that young," he said. "But I started earlier than most. I'm not as green as you think."

"Hell, you don't have to prove nothin' to me, son. I'm not the one who hired you to watch the small-town cops in over their head."

"No, no. It's not like that. Just think of me as part of the team, but focused on this one particular case."

Sheriff Mason looked Damon up and down again. He smiled.

"Look, I'll take it! Sorry about the poor introduction. Can never be too sure, ya know. But you're right. We don't really get cases like this, and my guys aren't all that experienced to crack it. I mean, domestic disturbance, vandalism, theft, yeah. But I'm still shook that this is happening, honestly. We take care of our own. Even more so, if he truly was taken, it was most likely by someone in this community. Someone we go to church with. Someone who's waited right in line next to us at the coffee shop. Or even in the PTA."

"Wait. What do you mean, if he truly was taken?" Damon asked.

"I mean, I think you ought to look at this not so much as lining up townspeople searching for suspects, and more ask the right questions to dig into the truth. Be open to all possibilities."

Damon gave him a puzzled look. Did the sheriff know more than what he was letting on?

Sheriff Mason rolled his eyes. "Here's the thing," he said as he opened the desk drawer and pulled out the file for the missing boy. He tossed it onto the desk with a smack. "There's no inclination that he was ever taken. His so-called disappearance from the O'Leary household doesn't line up. No one entered or exited the home except for the father heading to work. The video doorbell footage didn't see anything. We even checked the feed from the neighbors. The window to the bedroom is right in front, so even if he'd left through there, we'd have captured it. We swept the river and woods nearby the house. You see what I'm getting at?"

"So, what do you think happened?"

"Well personally, I think it's either the O'Learys themselves, or the kid ran away. The parents are having marital problems. When I questioned the O'Leary woman, she said as much. You want to start? Go investigate the home where the kid was taken. Press them a bit. The parents are all old friends, so we didn't hold them to the flame too much after initial questioning, but I think there's more there. Or hell, maybe they're all in on it and merely want some attention and internet fame. You remember that bubble boy?"

"You mean balloon boy?"

"That's the one. I hate even going down that route of thinking. But these days you just never know. Ya know?"

"Mhm," Damon said, humoring the sheriff. It began to sink in there wasn't much of an investigation to get caught up to speed on. "Anything else I should know?"

Sheriff Mason looked lost in thought for a second before perking up to answer.

"Yeah. Well, just some advice, I guess. I'ma let you know right now, no one in town will wanna talk to you. Not really. It's not that they don't want to help find the boy, but they really stick to their own. If you're gonna be here, and want to feel like you're being cooperated with, make sure you involve yourself a bit. Get to know them. Don't stay at that damn Motel 6 or Marriott off the interstate. There's a bed and breakfast in town that would have room for you. You can stay there. Tell them Sheriff Mason sent you and they'll give you a little discount. Spend some time downtown and weave yourself into the community. It'll pay dividends. You a religious man?"

Damon hadn't even thought about it in quite a while.

"Not thoroughly devout, I guess. Should probably go to

church more than I do."

"Good. Sunday service, whole town damn near shuts down. Again. It's important to the community. It should be important to you. Pastor Bettany is long winded, but his message always seems to hit home."

"Thanks. But I don't think I'll still be here, then. Not if we can find Adam as soon as we should."

Sheriff Mason looked at Damon and shrugged. "I'm just saying if."

CHAPTER TWENTY

Wyatt shambled into the kitchen and filled his thermos from the coffee pot as his truck warmed up in the driveway. He watched as his wife paced around him, collecting her things and looking prepared to rush out the door. "Where are you going so early?" he asked. In hindsight, he knew he should have at least led with "Good morning," but all chit-chat and small talk had been essentially nonexistent since Adam went missing. He was used to her being up and out of bed before him each day. What little broken pieces of sleep he'd been getting, she'd got even less. But normally she sat silently on the couch, staring off into the middle distance. This morning, she seemed to have a fire within her.

"Back to Marshport. I need to be there," Julie said. "Until I find or hear anything to make me think otherwise, our son is somewhere in that town. Or at least someone must know something. I never got a chance to actually hand out the fliers or talk to anyone, because of going to the school. Which, by the way, I never got a chance to ask—how could you not pick him up? I was all the way out there."

"I was working. Sorry. By the time I saw the missed calls, you were already on your way."

"Working," she said dismissively. "I don't see how you can

even go in to work. Not with everything going on."

He screwed the lid onto his thermos. "I already missed the first half of the week. But I took all my PTO during the summer. I didn't think I'd have to . . ." He trailed off, unable to finish the thought out loud.

"They'd surely understand and—"

"And what, Julie? Give me some unpaid leave? Hold my job for me? That would be great. Sure. So I can do what? Sit around here in a fog like you? Think of all the 'what if' scenarios that don't really matter? Jules, if I don't keep busy, I'll lose my goddamned mind. What the hell would you rather I do?"

"I'd rather you not walk around and go about your day like everything is normal, for one!"

"Excuse me? What makes you think I'm doing anything normal?"

"Really? You wake up and shower and head out to work like everything is fine. Then come home and want to talk about your stupid day over dinner. Meanwhile I am doing whatever I can to find our son and put our family back togeth —"

"Oh, that's fucking rich. Now you're the one that cares about our family?" he blurted out. He didn't mean to, and regretted it immediately.

Julie leaned forward and narrowed her eyes into red-hot daggers.

"Are you seriously making this about you and me right now?" she asked.

Wyatt shook his head and kneaded the back of his neck. "No. Of course not. But don't stand there and come at me like you're more worried about Adam than I am. Like it's some fucking competition. That's sick, Jules. The police and an investigator that we hired are all searching for him. What can you do that they can't?"

"How can you do anything but look for our son? You gonna

go in the garage later and screw around in the truck? Build a table or something? How? Why?"

Wyatt watched as her whole body melted. Her fury dissipated as her shoulders dropped, and she sank into herself.

She softly muttered, "Nothing but this matters anymore."

"I don't know if you've noticed," Wyatt said, "but we still have another son that needs us too. Now more than ever." He spoke low, but sharply through gritted teeth, so Stephen wouldn't hear them. "So one of us has to try and not totally detach from the world. Not to mention, I can't even step foot in the town, or that Kirk guy will have me arrested, which is one reason we hired Damon in the first place." He left the kitchen into the dining room, trying but failing to walk away from the conversation.

Julie marched behind him. "Don't do that. Don't make me the bad guy, here."

Wyatt turned to face her again. She bit her bottom lip as it quivered.

"It's your fault he's gone," she said, removing all air from the dining room.

"Wh-what?" Wyatt stuttered. "How can you—"

She gripped the back of the wooden chair and leaned forward. "He called you! He called us that night, and said he wanted to come home. Your son needed you, and you told hi —"

"Don't you think I know that?" he yelled back. "That that's all I can think about? That I can hear his voice over and over and over. But it was almost two in the morning, Julie. And we'd been drinking. Don't you think I have that eating away at me every goddamned minute of the day? How I lost one of the most important things in my life trying to save . . . you know what? Never mind. I have to go to work so we can pay for the PI you demanded we hire."

Wyatt stormed toward the front door and ripped his keys off the wall hanger. The last thing he heard was "Wyatt, wait I didn't—" as he slammed the door behind him on the way out.

***

Julie hopped in her car with her mind still racing.

Before she knew it, she sat in the parking area for the Marshport Town Square and pavilion area, filled with determination and hyperfocus. She exited the SUV and stapled missing child posters to the bulletin board and on posts at each corner. She passed out the remaining papers to passersby on the street. A young woman dog walking grabbed a flier with her free hand as she walked by. Julie handed one each to a young couple who looked to be heading to school.

"Please," she said. "If you see or hear anything or have any information that could help, please call the number at the bottom."

"For sure," one of them said.

"We will," added the other.

She canvassed the area and continued handing out the fliers until something stopped her cold. Something that made her leap out of her skin. Her gaze darted around looking for an immediate answer, but there was none. She initially spotted only the corner of it, but she knew exactly what it was. One of her fliers was lying in the trash can beside the gazebo.

Julie pulled it from the trash to find a discarded hunk of chewing gum pressed into Adam's chest. It had then been folded in half and tossed into the receptacle. She sat on the gazebo steps, and her face collapsed into her hands.

"Mrs. Newcommer, can I sit down next to you, dear?"

Julie looked up and saw an older woman standing before her. She appeared to be in her early sixties, with short hair that Julie could tell was styled with home curlers.

"Umm . . . yeah," Julie said. "I'm sorry. Do I know you?"

"No. Probably not. But I own a bakery around the corner, and I was part of the search party for Adam. My name is

Carol." She sat down beside Julie and put her arm around her. "I can't stop thinking about Adam and how strong you are. Have you eaten?"

"No," Julie said. "I'm not hungry."

"Oh, nonsense. You can't starve yourself on top of everything else. Come with me. We'll get you something warm to drink, too."

Carol attempted to grab the stack of fliers, but Julie tightened her grip. The woman let go and smiled warmly.

"I'm so sorry," Carol said. "I didn't mean anything by it. Just trying to help you up."

"No, I'm sorry," Julie said, biting her lip.

"Oh, don't be. Not at all."

Julie walked beside her to her shop and stood awkwardly while Carol unlocked the front door. The inside was slightly cluttered but not unorganized. It felt warm and inviting, like a grandmother's kitchen more than the cold, fluorescent, corporate coffee shops she was used to.

"Eclair or fritter?" Carol asked.

"Oh, um . . . fritter."

"Vanilla or caramel creamer?

"Huh?

"For the coffee, dear. Vanilla or caramel creamer?"

"Caramel, please. Thank you." As Julie waited, she wandered the front of the bakery, looking in the glass cases and reading, but not at all retaining, the full menu of items. She looked over the committee-approved fliers displayed by the register, asking for purchases of popcorn tins to help the local scout troop, and donations toward new Christmas lights for the town square.

"Do you mind if I hang this flier up on your front door?" Julie asked. "I have approval."

Carol looked confused, then rolled her eyes. "Oh, you must have talked to Gregory. Of course you can." The smell of baked goods and roasted coffee filled the shop as she emerged from behind the counter holding the white ceramic plate and steaming mug. "But first, come over here and sit down. There's no easy way to say this, but I beg you to listen." She guided Julie over to a small corner table and put Julie's hands in her own. Carol took a deep breath, then paused. "You and your family need to stay away from here. Nothing good can come from it."

"What?" Julie choked out. "I'm here searching for my son. How can you say that?"

"Oh, I understand. I can't imagine what you're going through."

"Why does everyone keep saying that?" Julie asked.

Carol continued on without acknowledgment. "And I pray for you and your family every day. But something is angered, and it reigns over that house. Stay away from it." She looked over at the front door, then back to Julie. "I feel for you all, I really do. I'm only trying to help. But there's a presence over that house. I don't know why your son was chosen. But he was. He isn't the first. That girl dying was no accident, I can promise you that."

"Carol, I appreciate the breakfast, but if you think that little girl—"

"It wasn't just the girl! There have been others. I tried to tell Kirk to stop renting that place out. But he's stubborn. He says it's not connected, but there's no coincidence. Says it's been in his family for generations, and since it's a Marshport historical landmark, they won't do anything about it. It's irresponsible. I said he should turn it into a museum or something if he doesn't want it to sit dormant. At least we wouldn't have to worry about people living there."

"I'm sorry, but I'm not just going to leave. My son is out there somewhere."

"Please. I realize what I'm asking. But before anything else bad happens—the more you tempt fate, the worse it gets. It's the curse of this town. The house no one wants to trick or treat at. There are so many tales told about it you can't keep track of what's real and what's not. No one really talks about it— they can't fathom our perfect little town having such a glowing black eye. But it isn't just stories and urban legends. I've seen it, dear. I've lived here a long time. I thought when it sat so long after the last time, Kirk finally came to his senses. But here we are. And so quickly, it happened again. Before I could even warn your friend. And I know you don't want to believe it. I know how everything in your body screams what I'm saying isn't real. But I've also noticed you haven't blinked. And your knuckles are white from gripping that mug so tightly. A piece of you knows it may be true. So please. I'm begging you. I'm trying to help."

Julie loosened her choke hold on the coffee mug and wiped her mouth with the napkin.

"Thank you, um, for the breakfast. But to be clear, nothing more can happen to me than has already happened." She began to sweat as the blood rushed back to her veins and her breath regulated. "The apple fritter was delicious."

Julie exited the bakery and ran face first into Gregory. He was in a group with a few others she didn't immediately recognize.

"Oh, my. That could have been a catastrophe," Gregory said. "Mrs. Newcommer, where are you going in such a hurry? We actually saw the two of you come in here, and it made me remember that I haven't had one of Carol's famous lemon squares in forever. So, we thought it would be the perfect place for us to discuss this week's Bible study. But also, we wanted to share that we are holding a support rally for your son right here in the town square."

"Oh, you guys have already done so much," Julie said. "I really gotta go. I need to . . . I just need to go."

"Oh, Mrs. Newcommer, please. Galatians 6:2? 'Bear one another's burdens, and so fulfill the law of Christ.' We feel we are all not only partly responsible, but also getting your son home will have everyone breathing a little easier."

"Come in and talk with us," a woman said, poking her head out from behind Gregory. "We really feel like we can help. Our mission is to get your son home."

"Adam," Julie said. "His name is Adam. I'm sorry, who are you?" She shook her head. "Never mind. I really have to go. And we will find him."

"Oh, don't worry about it. I'm Gloria. I was with your husband during the search, so we haven't officially met. And of course, if he's out here, we'll find him. For the rally, we're going to have vendors and food trucks and a hotline and brainstorming groups."

"Come and sit with us," another said. "We all must do what is necessary to keep Marshport safe. My name is Sherri. Sherri Langford. I own the bed and breakfast 'round the way. It's historic, ya know?" She pulled Julie by the arm and sat her down at the table with them. "Now, of course, we will have a funnel cake truck, but is your son more of a mac-and-cheese lover or a hot dog lover?"

Julie blinked repeatedly with her mouth agape. "I'm sorry. What?"

The bell on the door rang as it flew open.

"Julie!" Corrine said as she entered. "I've been trying to get a hold of you."

"Fucking unreal," Julie said. Her temples pulsed. "I gotta go. I appreciate you all, and anything you do to help locate my son, I wholeheartedly support." She rifled through her purse and pulled out three twenty-dollar bills, placing them on the counter.

"Mrs. Newcommer?" Carol said.

"Carol, I'd like to pick up their breakfast. Whatever is left, keep for yourself."

"Jules—" Corrine started.

Julie looked her way and shook her head dismissively. She rushed out of the bakery, almost shoving her friend aside on the way by. She walked at just a beat below a jog back to her car and slipped inside.

There, she cranked up the radio, blasting the heavy metal through the speakers. A coping mechanism she'd used back when her parents split up, one she'd recently adopted once again. She leaned the car seat back as far as it reclined and reached for a sweatshirt Stephen had recently left in the back seat. She covered her face with it, pressing it into her eyes. It was as close as she could get to pausing the world and escaping the current plane of existence, even for just a little bit. Once she felt ready to continue, she took a few more deep breaths and slowly sat back up. She looked out. Exiting the sheriff's station, and heading her way, was Damon.

"Mrs. Newcommer. Good morning," he said.

"Oh, Jesus, Damon. My name is Julie," she said. "Please call me that. I'm not your kindergarten teacher."

"Will do. I just got done talking to the sheriff. I already see where some of your concerns stemmed from. He's there now if you were here to touch base with him."

"Oh, I'm not." She looked over at the station and winced. "I don't think that's a good idea. Our last couple interactions haven't gone well. You'll get further with him without me. I actually think . . . yeah. I'm gonna make some more fliers. And walk the woods and river again. So, if you need or find anything, I'll be close."

"Sounds good. I also decided I'm going to be staying in town. Heading to the bed and breakfast right now."

Julie turned to walk away before spinning back around. "Actually, before you do that, you may want to head to the bakery."

He nodded. "I'll be sure to do that."

<u>CHAPTER TWENTY-ONE</u>

Damon walked the streets of the Marshport town square. After spending the afternoon getting settled in and attempting to speak to some of the locals, it seemed like most of the residents had slowly but surely left him all alone. The purple-yellow dusk began casting shadows against the trees and businesses. Earlier today, the area had held steady foot traffic, but it all felt eerily still as he wandered in solitude.

He turned a corner and noticed a few people conversing at the bottom of the small set of concrete steps of the church. They looked up at him, probably because he casually turned the corner and came to a dead stop. But they quickly went back to whatever it was they talked about. The bells rang with a loud, echoing clang, and the people stopped midconversation and hustled inside. Damon looked at his watch. It was 7 p.m. He walked toward the church and followed them in.

He expected to see the most devout of the town attending their second service of the week. Yet instead of the pews filling, they were piling into the church gymnasium.

White plastic folding chairs were lined in rows with a walkway down the middle. Damon took a seat in the back corner of the room. In front of the chairs, a long folding table sat a handful of people, one of whom was Sherri. He'd met her earlier when checking into the bed and breakfast. Most of the rest he'd also seen at the bakery this morning. He jotted down notes from what he could pick up.

Someone crept by him, scanning over the chairs for a place to sit. Damon gently tugged on the sleeve of the man's leather jacket. "Excuse me," he said. "What is this?"

"Who are you?" the man asked. He smelled of aftershave, and the scally cap on top of his head had begun to fray at the seams.

Before Damon could respond, the man was hurried along by someone else.

"C'mon, we gotta find a seat. Don't want to get called out in front of everyone," they said as they unwound the knit scarf from their neck and stuffed it into their coat pocket as best they could. The two rushed away and sat a few rows forward.

As people took their seats, a tall, bearded man in a sweater vest approached the podium and tapped the microphone. The reverberating thumps from the tapping bookended the high-pitched squeal screaming from the speakers.

"Geez, Gregory, we see you up there. The mic thing is unnecessary!" one of the residents yelled.

"I just wanted to make sure I had your attention," Gregory said. "All right guys, Gloria is running a little bit late. And then we will get the town meeting started. Feel free to grab some snacks, once again graciously donated by Carol's Bakery."

"I'm here, I'm here," Gloria said as she rushed in the door and up to the podium. Even though everyone had already stopped talking and turned their attention up front when she approached, she banged the wooden gavel on the podium top. "Good evening, everyone. I'm glad to see yet another great turnout. It shows how much you all care about and want to make this community great. First order of business. Planning for the Fourteenth Annual Cow Plop should be started soon. Now, I stand by my opinion that this is beneath us," she said with a shudder. "But you all seem to love it, and it raises a good deal of money for the school."

Damon leaned forward and whispered to the couple ahead of him, "I'm sorry. What's she talking about?"

"The cow plop," one of them answered. "It's silly, but we do it every year. We borrow a cow from Sawyer Farm and leave her on the fifty-yard line of the high school football stadium. We sell tickets to the event, and all place bets on where the cow will, well . . . plop."

"I'm sorry, am I boring you?" Gloria said.

"No, Gloria, he was asking me—"

"It's rude to— Wait, I'm sorry. Who are you?" she said, looking to Damon. "Town hall meetings are for Marshport residents only."

So much for keeping a low profile, Damon thought to himself.

"Yes, I understand that," he said. "Hi, everybody. My name is Damon Williams. I'm helping the Newcommers find their son, Adam. I'm sure you all have heard about him going missing by now?"

"Oh, I just feel so bad for them," someone said.

"Wait, you don't think Sheriff Mason is capable?" another asked.

The sheriff, who stood in the back corner of the gymnasium, smiled and held up his arms.

"Oh, it's not that," Damon said. "Just that the sheriff already has his hands full with the day-to-day stuff of the town. Wyatt and Julie wanted some extra help. I like to think I'm working with the sheriff."

"Who's Wyatt and Julie?" an older man asked.

"The parents of the missing boy, Harold. Keep up," said the woman sitting next to him.

The individual voices and questions shifted into a rolling

constant of white noise, and Damon struggled to keep up. Only a few stray comments popped out above the rest. He couldn't respond to a single one before another would jump out at him.

"Sheriff, did you know about this?"

"Are you retiring?"

"Should we be worried about our children?"

Sheriff Mason waved his arms over his head, commanding the attention of the gymnasium. Damon stopped thrashing water, thankful to get a moment's rest. Was every town-hall meeting like this, or just ones infiltrated by strangers?

"Now, now. You all can rest easy," the sheriff said. "I talked to Mr. Williams this morning, and we're going to work together to bring the missing boy back home. Truth is, we're a bit out of our element here, and some fresh eyes on the situation could prove crucial."

"You should start with the O'Leary parents," Gloria said. "I never trusted them from the minute they came into town. You can tell just by looking at them."

"It's not the parents. It's the house!" another said, his outburst commandeering everyone's attention more than the bright yellow Marshport Beautification Committee sweatshirt he wore. "Burn it down. Marshport would be better off."

"Randy, c'mon, this again? You trying to scare people?" Sheriff Mason asked.

"Scaring who? They all know it. You're the delusional one if you think otherwise. But we can't just pretend it doesn't exist."

Damon suddenly realized he was so busy absorbing everything happening around him, he hadn't been writing anything down. He reached into the inside pocket of his coat and pulled out a small notebook and pen.

Gloria smacked the gavel against the podium. "Can we please get back to the topic at hand, before our meeting was hijacked?"

"I'm sorry," Damon said. "Shouldn't this be the top priority?"

"The Marshport Historical Society does not step on the toes of law enforcement. We all have our part to play. But, Mr. Williams, as for our part, we were actually about to discuss the rally planning for the boy to brainstorm and raise awareness."

"Oh, for the love of—" Randy said, cutting her off. "You guys and your festivals. They're worthless. Self-congratulatory bullshit. No better than internet thoughts and prayers. The boy is gone." Randy gestured toward Damon. "Sorry to our PI friend here, but it's true. And it needs to stop here. Burn that beacon of evil to the ground! We can't allow it to invite any more of our kids to be swallowed whole!" Randy turned his attention to Kirk, who was seated at the head table next to Gregory with the other historical society members. "You should have had the damn thing demolished years ago! But you're greedy. It should have stopped after the girl. Look how quickly it's already happened again."

"Dammit, Randy. Do I have to take you in for public intoxication again?" asked the sheriff.

"I'm not drunk! Just the only one with some damned sense in this town. There's something evil there, and you all just pretend it doesn't exist. But you'll sure keep away from it. Why?"

Randy looked around the room with a face yearning for backup, yet he found only a room of people unwilling to acknowledge him at all. Most of them looked away as he tried to make eye contact. It was the first day, and Damon had already witnessed a hairline fracture in the tight community the sheriff bragged about.

Mason locked eyes with his officers and motioned his head toward Randy. Officer Daniels nodded and pushed himself off the wall he'd been leaning against.

"C'mon, let's go," Hewitt said as Daniels grabbed Randy

by the bicep. "We're gonna go downtown for a bit."

"Really? For what?" Randy said.

"Look around, Randy. You're disturbing the peace."

"No! You know I'm right! Don't let them take me!" He repeated this with increasing desperation and intensity. "Please don't let them take me."

"C'mon, Randy. Let's go relax a bit," Daniels said as he shoved open the gymnasium double doors with his back and led Randy outside to the squad car.

The door closed again with an echoey clang, which trailed off into complete silence from the group.

"C'mon, people. That's enough. Let's get back to what we were doin'," Sheriff Mason said, waving his arm around in a helicopter motion.

"I'm sorry. What girl?" Damon asked. His voice echoed inside the open gym, cutting through the crowd, who sat with awkward faces that answered more than they knew.

"Oh, nothin'. Don't even pay him any mind. It don't pertain to the case you're working. Just an unfortunate tragedy that the town has moved on from."

"Doesn't sound like everyone has moved on," Damon said. The way the crowd sat facing forward, either outright ignoring him or in a silent stalemate, wondering who would break and engage first, left Damon on an island. There was nothing more for him here tonight. He turned his attention to the front of the room. "It was nice to meet you all, but I'm going to head out. If any of you have any information about Adam, please call the number on the card. I'm going to leave a stack of them on the table here. I'll also be staying at the Stepford Bed and Breakfast."

CHAPTER TWENTY-TWO

Corrine pulled back the living room shade enough to peek out the window. It was just before four in the evening, and schoolchildren walked the streets without a care that a child had just disappeared on this very street. Connor had recently arrived home and was doing his homework at the kitchen table, a rule she enforced mainly to keep him from heading straight to his bedroom—not to be seen again until dinner, where he'd inhale some food and scurry right back into solitude once again.

Across the street, Herbert Wright raked up fallen leaves from his maple tree and struggled to get the piles into lawn bags. She'd have offered to help, but she knew he'd decline and find an excuse to retreat inside—either remembering the tea kettle was ready or the television was still on.

Two boys in scout uniforms rolled a cart from door to door, selling popcorn. She watched as they approached the end of her sidewalk, argued about something briefly, and played rock-paper-scissors. One boy celebrated while the other sank down before shaking his head and running down the street.

"Hey, wait up. Don't leave me here alone," the remaining boy yelled, following after.

Corrine felt like she watched as the rest of the world move

on without her. She had hoped with moving closer to the center of the town, she'd stop feeling like as much of an outsider. But those hopes had evaporated after Adam's disappearance. Now she received side-eyes and everyone mysteriously needing to rush off as soon as she attempted to strike a conversation at a shop or diner.

She placed an incense stick on the holder and patted the front of her charcoal-colored duster cardigan until the impression of the lighter reminded her which pocket it was in. She pulled it out and lit the end of the incense before waving her hand through the silky stream of smoke, wafting it into the living room air.

Corrine didn't leave the house much anymore, hoping to remain close and connect to some real evidence of Adam still being with them. Somehow. It was the only thing that made sense.

She walked into the kitchen, where Connor was sitting at the table, doing his homework.

"You like this one?" she asked. "It's Elecampane."

Connor scrunched his face. "Ugh. Not really. It stinks. Are you cooking mothballs?"

"Whatever. It should help. How was school today?"

He shrugged his shoulders.

"Everything okay?" she asked.

"I'm just worried about Adam."

"I know, babe. We all are." She kissed the top of his head and ran her fingers through his hair. "He will be back with us soon. I feel it."

"It's my fault, though. I shouldn't have fallen asleep on him. We were going to stay up all night."

"Don't say that. It's no one's fault," she said, though she herself felt the most guilty about him disappearing.

"The other kids at school are scared of me," Connor said in an almost disconnected monotone.

"What? Why?"

"They keep saying our family is cursed. Because of the house."

"Oh, that's nonsense. What do you think?" Corrine asked.

"I don't know. I want to go back to our old house."

"I know. But that's not an option right now. It's important that we hold tight." She pulled a stock pot from the cupboard and began filling it with water. "Spaghetti okay? It'd just be jar stuff. Your dad's working late. Again. So, it's just gonna be you and me."

"Yeah, that's fine. Do we have garlic bread?"

A knock came from the front door.

"Yeah, I think so. Can you grab that while I double-check?"

He jogged out of the kitchen toward as she pulled open the freezer. She moved around the pizza rolls and a package of chicken thighs, not finding any garlic bread to speak of.

"Mom, some dude is here!" Connor yelled from the other room.

She shook her head in frustration and mocked slamming her head in the freezer door.

"Okay!" she yelled back. She straightened her head scarf and draped the kitchen towel over her shoulder. As she passed Connor while heading to the door, she said in a low voice, "Who is it?"

He raised his eyebrows and shrugged his shoulders.

Corrine pulled open the door to reveal a man dressed head to toe in black, from the winter hat to the coat to the jeans and boots. His hands were in his pockets, but if he had gloves on, she figured they'd probably be black as well. The man bounced a bit upon being greeted, which snuffed the initial aura of mystery around him.

"Can I help you?" she asked.

"Hi, I'm Damon. Uh, Damon Williams. I'd like to ask some questions about the disappearance of Adam Newcommer."

"I'm sorry, who? I already told the police everything."

"Yeah, I know. I heard. I—"

"Are you from the press? This is a really hard time for us and—"

"The press?" he said, seemingly thrown off by the term. "No, the Newcommers hired me. I'm a private investigator."

Corrine blankly nodded as she wrung the kitchen towel around her hands. "Hold on," she said, and closed the door. She grabbed her phone off the wireless charger seated on the end table and frantically typed away.

There's a guy here asking questions and claims you hired him. Did you guys hire a PI?

In no time, her phone chirped a response.

It's been almost a week, and I'm no closer to finding Adam. Your Barney Fife cops are useless. I'd tell him everything you know. Unless you have something to hide.

Corrine rested her head against the back of the door. The cool steel soothed her as she took a deep breath and shook out her body, freeing the tears pushing themselves from the corners of her eyes. She swallowed hard and cleared her throat before opening the door again.

"Sorry. I just needed to verify with them that you're legit. You understand," she said.

Damon nodded. "Yes, ma'am."

Corrine opened the screen door and offered for him to come inside.

"Thank you," he said.

"Can I get you some tea or water or anything to drink?" she asked as she led him into the kitchen.

"No thanks. I'm good." He slid the kitchen chair back and took a seat. "Now, I—"

"Sorry. Give me just a second, actually." She dumped the box of spaghetti noodles into the pot of boiling water and sent Connor off to do his homework in the living room so the two could talk.

***

While he waited, it dawned on Damon where he recognized her from. Though, as she'd paid for her food and rushed out of the bakery, she'd seemed too upset at the time to approach. If he'd known her identity then, it might have changed his mind.

"I saw you at the coffee shop yesterday morning, actually. I don't know if you remember me. But it seemed like you were having a rough morning?" he said, unsure if it was even a question or not.

"No. Sorry, I don't remember you. But that? It was nothing. Really. Just a lot going on at the moment."

She came over and sat down beside Damon, folding her hands on the table.

"Mrs. O'Leary, I know you already talked to the Marshport Police," Damon said. "But can you walk me through the night of Adam's disappearance? Any detail, as insignificant as it may seem, could be a huge help in bringing him back home safely."

He thought it was a straightforward question, but Corrine instantly began to sob. Damon, while trying his best to remain professional, sat tall and wide-eyed, unsure of what to do.

"I don't know what happened," she said, her words crashing through like a dam that had burst. "I know how it looks. How it sounds. I'm aware. Of course I am. Every time I think back on that night, all the things that could have been done differently. I swear. I . . . I wish I could take it all back. Go back in time somehow and do it all over again. I love that boy. I wish—I just wish I knew what happened. Had some kind of an answer. Where he went. He's such a sweet boy. I can't imagine. I keep thinking about it over and over. Where he could have gone. If he went anywhere." She covered her palms with the wrist cuffs of her cardigan and pressed them against her eyes.

"Wh-what do you mean? Wish you could take what back?" he asked.

"Well, there's no sign of him even leaving. I mean, my husband was the only one to leave the house at all."

Damon wrote that down immediately.

"No, listen. Not like that. I've gone over that night a million times. And in my gut, with everything in me, I know he never left this house. He's still here. Somehow. I wish I could prove it. I didn't want to tell the sheriff, because I know how it sounds. I feel something heavy with this house. I didn't at first. But ever since that night, it just grows and grows."

Damon sat frozen with his pad open and pen on the page. He tapped the tip of the pen a couple times against the paper before shutting the notepad and sliding it off to the side.

"Mrs. O'Leary, with what has happened, do you actually feel safe with your family staying here?"

Corrine rolled her eyes upward and pursed her lips, seeming to meticulously search for the next words to say. After a moment, she leaned in toward Damon.

"I feel like us being here as a constant reminder is what will bring Adam back home safely. I half expect him to just walk down the hallway like nothing happened. Or look outside and he'll be sitting on the patio. We need to hold strong." She took a deep breath. "But we are moving Connor upstairs, and Phillip and I will take the bedroom down here. That's the project for the next couple days."

"Mrs. O'Leary, yo—"

"Corrine."

"Corrine, you've only been here for less than a month, correct? Can you tell me why you moved?"

"We needed a bit more space. I had talked to Kirk about wishing we were closer to the center of town; he mentioned he had this space available and said he'd work with us."

"So, he brought it up to you? Did he say how long it had been vacant?"

Instead of an answer, Damon's attention was seized by the stove flame roaring and climbing halfway up the stockpot from the pasta boiling over.

"Oh, dammit!" Corrine said as she shot up and killed the burner with a flick. She grabbed a wooden spoon and stirred the spaghetti, calming the foamed water. She popped open the sauce jar and dumped it into a second pot staged in front of her. As she worked the stove, she turned her head to face Damon. "Sorry. Umm, since, well, I think Ava's family were the last to live here. However long that was, exactly. You have heard about that, I'm assuming?"

Damon shifted his weight in the chair and sat up a bit straighter. He'd been wanting to poke her about this. Lucky for him, he didn't have to shoehorn a way to broach the topic. "Just bits and pieces. What actually did happen?"

"I heard she was climbing the closet shelves, trying to get a blanket or something, and they collapsed on her. Hit her head on the doorframe. She died instantly. The family moved away for a fresh start. That's just what I heard, anyway. It's hard to get actual information about it from anyone. They're all about keeping up appearances as the last great peaceful town in America."

"You don't like it here?"

"Oh, I love it here. But it definitely comes with people who kid themselves with how the world works and protect it with self-righteousness. To be honest, we don't really fit the mold here. But we try to get on well enough."

"Corrine, did you know that Adam called his parents and asked them to pick him up. Saying he was scared and couldn't sleep?"

"What?" she asked, sounding like the wind had escaped from her.

"It was . . ." Damon grabbed his notebook and flipped a few pages back, scanning with his index finger. "Close to 2 a.m. Do you know of any reason he'd ask to be picked up in the middle of the night?"

"I didn't know that. No, I don't."

"Nothing at all about that night? What about the next morning?"

"Again, I didn't get home until around one thirty or so. I checked on the boys, and Adam was still up."

"Did he seem upset, or anything that would raise a flag?"

"Um . . . no. No. I told them they needed to turn stuff off and get some sleep, because Julie was going to be here in the morning. And I didn't need her upset with me about letting her son stay up all night and being a zombie the next day. So, they turned stuff off and went to sleep. Or at least that's what I assumed."

"Then what did you do?"

"I went upstairs and went to bed. I was exhausted. I tried to have a glass of wine and watch a bit of TV, but was nodding off. That's the last thing I remember. I woke up the next day, and Julie got here soon after."

Damon looked over at the clock on the stove and ran his tongue across his molars. He couldn't help but hear some of the sheriff's words weave themselves into the front of his mind.

"Where's your husband?" he asked. "I'd love to talk to him as well. Try and learn anything from earlier in the evening."

"Oh, he's still on a job. He won't be back for a few hours, probably."

"What's he do exactly?"

"Plumber. Well, he owns his own business. On call twenty-four hours," she said in an uptick as if she didn't approve, but had no choice. "It's how we can afford to stay here, really."

He scratched his neck, just below his ear. "Does he often leave in the middle of the night?"

"Not normally. But sometimes he needs to leave early depending on the drive. He has a lot of connections still from the city that refer him." She chuckled before adding," People love supporting a small business. He had an early Sunday-morning appointment for a burst pipe."

Damon flipped through his notes again. "I thought it was a well pump."

"Maybe. I zone out on the details, really. Whatever he said is probably what it was. I know it was a big project that he was leaving early for."

He stood up and pushed his chair back in.

"Oh, was that all?" Corrine asked.

"Actually, do you mind if I have a look around? I'd love to see the bedroom?"

They left the kitchen and walked down the hallway. Connor's room met them at a dead end at the end of the hall. The hollow wooden door creaked as Corrine swung it open and gestured for Damon to enter. He wandered around, unsure what he was searching for, just looking. He walked up to the bedroom closet and looked inside.

"Does your son know about the girl's death?"

"I'm not sure. We've never really talked about it. Just something that happened. But we see death as just the next phase of being. Not the depressive finality other do. It's something that we're all very open to, actually."

Damon nodded in agreement, though his mind screamed otherwise. He walked to the bedroom window and noticed it was locked.

"The reports from that night said no one entered or exited through the doors. But there's no sensors on the windows. Could he have been taken through there?"

"No, I always make sure they're locked. With the master bedroom being the loft upstairs, I'm paranoid about it. I check every night."

"Okay, but could Adam have left on his own accord?"

"What?"

"Could he have climbed out of the window without anyone knowing?"

"Why would he do that?"

"Well, I heard he was being bullied. His parents were fighting and discussing separation. He tried to have them come pick him up and they didn't. Maybe that was the last straw to him running away. I've seen kids do it over less."

"Yeah, but all his stuff was left here," she said. "Even the phone."

"Yeah. That's odd. But if he didn't want to be found, he wouldn't take the phone. Right?" He gave the window a tug, even though it was locked, and it unsurprisingly didn't budge.

"Or shoes? In October?" Corrine said.

Damon wandered back toward the bedroom closet. "True."

"Why do you keep going over there?" Corrine asked.

"I just keep thinking about that little girl. That would be terrible."

"It's not that one. It's the hall closet."

She led him out of Connor's room and down the hallway. Much like the bedroom closet, this didn't seem like much of anything extraordinary. Some towels and toiletries. The vacuum. Winter boots. Damon put his hand out in front of him, feeling the closet air.

"Yeah, it gets cold. More so at night," Corrine said, answering Damon's question before he could ask it. "I'm telling you; it's them. I just know it."

Damon flashed a half smile of acknowledgment. He grabbed one of the shelves firmly and shook it. It didn't budge.

"Kirk said the whole thing was rebuilt," Corrine said. "'Overconstructed' was the term he used. Said he never wanted that to happen again. He holds himself responsible, even though it was an accident. But he was also very adamant my son knew to not climb on the shelves."

"Mhm," Damon said. He half listened to Corrine, but something about what stood before him felt off. "Is there a light in here?"

"No, not in the closet."

Damon used the flashlight on his phone and shined it around the inside. With the other hand, he felt up and down the side walls.

"What are you doing?" Corrine said.

"It's not just cold. You can feel it. Drafty." Damon shined the flashlight along the wall once more before clicking it off. "You got a lighter or candle or something?"

Corrine pulled the lighter from her cardigan and handed it to him. Damon held it against the wall by the shelves, and the flame flickered and waved. He left it lit and slowly slid it up and down the wall, watching as the flame waved from side to side but didn't blow out.

"Shit!" he yelled as he dropped the lighter and the room went dark again.

Corrine jumped backward. "Oh my god. What is it?"

"Nothing," Damon said, shaking out his hand. "Just held the lighter on too long. Burned my thumb. Sorry." He slid the towels aside and knocked on the wall. It responded with a deep, echoey thud.

"What's behind this?" he asked.

"Nothing in the house. The laundry cutout in the kitchen butts up to it, I guess."

"I don't think . . ." He trailed off without finishing the thought. Knocking again, he heard the same hollow feedback. He pulled the towels and blankets from the shelves and handed them to Corrine. "Hold these," he said, and began to knock along the wall, back and forth, listening for any variation, but it all gave the same sound. He took the side of his fist and slammed it, cratering a spot in the drywall.

"What are you doing?" Corrine yelled.

Damon didn't answer. Instead, he punched again, this time leaving a hole big enough to shine the light in and look inside. The open space behind the wall was dark and empty. Dust particles floated in the air, glistening in the beam of the flashlight.

"Call the police," he said.

CHAPTER TWENTY-THREE

When Sheriff Mason arrived at the O'Leary house, his officers had already responded and arrived on the scene. The neighbors stood on their front lawns in true rubbernecking fashion.

"Will you all go back inside your homes?" Mason called out to them. He shook his head and muttered to himself, "For cripes' sake."

He knocked on the screen door. "Hello?" he said, projecting his voice deep into the threshold before he walked right in.

One of the officers approached the sheriff as he entered. He scratched the back of his head and stood before Mason with his mouth hanging open. "Uhh . . . Sheriff, you'll wanna check this out. It's pretty weird."

"Daniels, you are an officer of the law. How about you not describe things as 'weird' and you investigate instead?"

"Yes, sir."

He wasn't sure exactly what kind of scene he was walking into, but he knew ahead of time that Damon had stumbled onto what he thought was a huge break in the case. Mason felt bad, but only slightly. It was a shame he'd have to bring him crashing down to earth. He wasn't a bad kid, just in over his head. The couch was piled high with contents the sheriff guessed used to fill the hallway closet. Inside the closet, in the back wall, was a hole cut out big enough for a person the size of Damon to climb through. Sheriff Mason's broader frame didn't stand a chance, however. He smirked when he saw the private investigator rotating in the dark, using his phone as a flashlight.

"What'd you find, son?" Mason asked with his face in the torn-out drywall.

"What do you mean, 'what did I find'? There's a secret room behind the hall closet."

"I see that." Sheriff Mason leaned back and stretched his neck into the hallway toward his officers. "Hey Daniels, call Kirk. He needs to know what's happening before the gossipers get word to him and he gets all startled. Let him know I'm here."

***

Damon instantly felt defensive seeing the sheriff immediately blow the whole thing off. He seemed to be consistent about that. Must be easy in a town like this.

"How are you not freaking out about this," Damon asked. "Did you know about it?"

"Dammit, Williams, will you listen to me? Alright, if you look up in the corner, there's gonna be a handle or rope or something. Look for that."

Damon shined his light along the back of the wall, and his face sank. He looked through the hole toward the sheriff, then back up to the corner. He reached up and grabbed the handle screwed into the two by fours framing the inside of the wall. He pushed out, but the wall didn't budge.

"Oh, it's uh, it's the other way," Mason said.

Damon pulled and heard a click before the entire closet back wall swung open, offering an entrance to the O'Learys' closet and into the hallway.

"Oh, hello, Sunshine," Sheriff Mason said, smiling.

"You knew about this?"

"Course I did. Marshport is an old prohibition town. The river extends out to the lake, and they used to run alcohol all through here. This ain't the only house with something like this either. The Newtons have a bookcase that slides along the wall, exposing a wine cellar behind it. Hell, why don't you go smash all their windows." Mason shined his light to the top of the door. "Look, the release is on both sides, so crashing through the wall was especially unnecessary. Did you even talk to Kirk like I said to? He ain't really keeping it a secret. It's a neat little quirk."

Sheriff Mason turned to Corrine.

"We'll be out of your hair in just a minute Mrs. O'Leary," he said. "Sorry about the fuss. If Kirk didn't tell you about that, I'll give him the riot act."

Damon turned off the phone light and slipped it back into his pocket. The way the sheriff seemed to thrive on shooting him down, almost to the point of humiliation, already grew tiresome. That toothy, condescending grin quickly made Damon's blood boil.

"Well, your guys didn't seem to know about it either," Damon said. "And when we were going over the case, and the evidence, and the questioning, you didn't even think to mention it? How are you treating this hidden room, in the house where a child went missing, like a non-fucking-factor?"

Sheriff Mason spun back around, his face filled with resentment. Damon could tell he'd struck a nerve, and the sheriff wasn't having fun anymore.

"Cuz it wasn't a factor," he said. "And while I understand you're not under my employment, I'd advise you to watch your tone and your language. Look, it's all sealed off," he said, shining his flashlight around the inside of the closet. "They all are. But back in the day, this used to be the speakeasy. That there is common knowledge. I didn't think you'd lose your mind and start tearing the damn house apart. I told you, before you play Superman, you need to learn some history on this town and the community. It really behooves you to—"

"Don't talk down to me like I'm out of line here. I am the only person who I know, for a fact, has nothing to do with the disappearance of Adam Newcommer. For all I know, you're hiding something too!"

"Now wait just a damn minute, son. I will not have you throwing stones and baselessly attacking people looking for answers. That is not how things are done in my town."

"Sheriff, I will tear this whole town apart if I have to while you nonchalantly mosey your ass around hoping to stumble into the poor kid. There's a sense of urgency necessary here that none of you seem to have. And I can clearly see why I'm here. So, if you aren't going to help me, I will go above, under, and through you to find this child."

Sheriff Mason stared at Damon as he slid his flashlight back into his belt.

"I think you should go," he said. "You've done enough here tonight."

Damon snatched his coat from the back of the couch. He walked with his chest out and his shoulders square until he knew he was out of sight from Sheriff Mason, and then his posture all but crumbled. It wasn't just the fact he'd torn the O'Learys' house apart for nothing that weighed on him. He didn't even care that he'd surely have to pay for damages to the closet. It was that he'd been so sure. So sure he was on to something, just to come up short. It wasn't the first time. His uncle had made that clear recently.

As he almost reached the front door, Corrine ran up and stopped him.

"Mr. Williams. Mr. Williams!"

"I'm sorry about this. But . . . but I just—" He shook his head and walked out.

Corrine followed him out the door. "I didn't know about the room. I don't know if it was common knowledge around the town. But Kirk never disclosed that. I would have— I mean I wouldn't have—"

"Good night, Mrs. O'Leary. If you think of anything else about that night, do not hesitate to call me." Damon handed her his card and slumped into his car.

The curiosity outside had died down and the onlookers had mostly recoiled back into their homes, leaving only the misty early-evening air and the sheriff's red and blue lights painting the O'Learys' front lawn as he drove away, dejected, heading back to the Stepford Bed and Breakfast, the place he currently called home.

CHAPTER TWENTY-FOUR

Damon spent the early portion of the next morning in the dining area of the inn. He poked around at his pancakes and scrambled eggs and sausage patties while replaying the previous night in a continuous loop.

When the breakfast food stopped distracting him, he focused on the vintage decor. The green and violet floral wallpaper, the sconces hanging equidistantly along the wall. Framed autographed pictures of celebrities who had stayed there over the years adorned the walls along the staircase, inviting admiration as guests climbed to their rooms.

At the bottom of the stairwell hung a disturbingly beautiful painting of a small ram trapped in a bush. Beside the bush was an angel yelling at an old man—some odd thrift store find or old family possession, he assumed. The entire lobby and lounge area smelled of clean linen. Not the actual aroma of fresh laundry, but the artificial fragrance used in candles and plug-in air fresheners.

Something Sheriff Mason had said rang repeatedly in Damon's head. *Embrace the community. Learn the history of the town.*

"Excuse me, Sherri," he said to the owner as she vacuumed around the questionably carpeted dining area. "Say I were trying to learn a little more about Marshport . . . do you have any suggestions of where to start?"

"What, like places to eat and see? You don't like my breakfast?"

"No, I'm sorry. Your breakfast is great," he said, cramming a forkful of pancakes and sausage into his mouth. "Sweet and savory. Just like I like it." He swallowed it all down. "No, umm . . . like about the town itself, I guess."

"You kids don't use Google anymore? I just can't keep up."

"Yeah, but—" Damon started to say, but she just continued on.

"You're gonna venture out today? It's supposed to storm. Well, I guess the community center would have some decent information. But really, your best bet would probably be the library. They've got an entire corner dedicated to the town. The history. The famous visitors. How the whole thing turned around from swampland to just the nicest little place. But honey, you got a few hours yet. The library doesn't open until ten. It's barely after seven-thirty."

Damon looked at his cell phone and then back up at Sherri.

"Oh, jeez. What time did I get down here, even?"

"Not sure exactly. But I do know I fired up the grill early just for you, so if you don't eat them eggs, we're gonna have words."

"Yes, ma'am," he said sheepishly.

***

The library was walking distance from the bed and breakfast, as was almost everything worth doing in Marshport. Damon stopped into the coffee shop on the way and grabbed a vanilla latte and a blueberry scone. He didn't have the heart to tell Sherri, but her eggs were bland, and the lack of hot sauce made the whole thing borderline inedible.

While he waited for his food, two women stood side by side

in line, leaning on strollers as they conversed in a hushed tone. One glanced over at him, leaned over, and whispered something to the other. They both looked his way, failing to be discreet. When they noticed Damon had spotted them, they turned away again.

The barista called his name, and he grabbed the food and rushed out. Without looking back as he exited, Damon still felt most of the coffee shop staring at him. That feeling stayed with him as he traveled the rest of the way to the library.

"Good morning," he said to the librarian as he approached the desk. She was younger, in her late teens or early twenties. Her legs were folded in front of her as she sat in the desk chair, and she read from a book nesting in the makeshift cradle of her lap.

"Can you tell me where the—" He stopped, spotting something in the corner. "Oh, never mind. I found it."

She raised her eyebrows and continued reading as he walked away.

The section sat under a banner reading "Welcome to Marshport!" and styled similarly to the overly decorative signs at the entrances to the town. There was also an intricate diorama of the town square area, reflecting all the current businesses, along with the dog park and gazebo.

He glossed over the obvious self-congratulatory junk food of picture books featuring famous visitors and origin stories of annual festivals. Many of the books, however, focused on the town's rich history. They detailed how, soon after the abolishment of prohibition, the town sought to expand and emulate larger Ohio cities like Cincinnati and Columbus. This continued for decades before ballooning crime rates and population decline shifted their values and approach. The book contained dated photos of the bed and breakfast, Hilltop Bar, Marshport Community Center, and a few other undisclosed buildings.

He stared at the picture of the bar. The front face looked

slightly different, but he still recognized it all the same. It was the house that the O'Learys now called home. He flipped back and forth through the pages, but after not finding what he was looking for, he carried the open book to the front desk and spun it around to face the librarian.

"Hi," he said. "This is probably going to sound like a weird question. Especially because you don't know me. But how much do you know about this town?"

"I know it's boring as hell," she said, barely looking up from her book.

"Did you grow up here?"

"In the library? Like some weird Hunchback of Notre Dame knockoff?"

"No, ugh . . . do you know why the Hilltop Bar was turned into a house?"

"Chill out, man. I'm just messing with you. Yeah, they renovated it after it caught fire. Don't know exactly when. But a long time ago. Why you asking?" She sat up and closed her book, keeping her index finger between the pages to hold her place. "Isn't that where that boy just went missing?"

"Yes, that's why I'm here."

"Oh, you're that guy?" she said as she nodded, and then chuckled. "Funny, you don't seem crazy."

"Is that what's already being said?"

"Don't respect the community or care about the people is what I heard. Good for you, man!"

"Thanks, I guess."

"I also heard you looked like a tall toddler. But I don't think that's true either."

Damon shook his head. "Listen, do you have a microfiche reader?"

She stared at him blankly.

"The thing to read old papers and—"

"Oh, the newspaper thingy! Yeah, it's over there," she said, pointing to the side wall behind a section of fantasy novels.

"Thanks," he said.

As he walked away, the girl chimed in again.

"Hey, since you brought it up, I'm not sure what is going on with that house. That place gives me the fucking creeps, though. Hilltop House is what all the kids called it growing up. I remember it being empty a lot."

Damon half smiled in acknowledgment as he continued to walk away.

Using the microfiche, he frantically scrolled through headline after headline from the Marshport Tribune, much of it pertaining to the goings-on in the town. The high school football team going to state. Fundraisers and festivals, of which there seemed to be plenty, all of them coordinated by the Marshport Historical Society.

Damon leaned back in the desk chair and rubbed his eyes before getting close again and staring at the screen. As he zoned out, he repeatedly, and at an increasing speed, tapped the desk with the tip of his middle finger.

He scribbled down some notes and scrolled back to the time around Ava's death. To his surprise, it wasn't in the paper as much as he would have thought. Small stories about the accident, but the front-page news of that day was about the expansion to the town square and the opening of a new corner store. He read through the article itself but only found mostly what was stated in the report and what the sheriff had additionally disclosed.

The few pictures he stumbled upon were from the memorial itself. Even in black and white, Ava's grief-stricken parents stuck out from what seemed to be the Marshport mold. The father had gauged earrings and a tattoo of kanji lettering surrounded by flames on the right side of his neck. The mother's bottom lip and septum were pierced, and even at the memorial she wore thigh-high, heeled black boots. Their names were not stated anywhere in the article. Only Ava's. They were merely listed as "survived by her mother and father." Damon scrolled back and forth around that date but found nothing about Ava after the article about the memorial.

He focused on the picture, as if trying to will it into telling him secrets. He slid over to a nearby computer and searched "The Hilltop." The search returned a lot of unnecessary information. He tried again, this time typing "The Hilltop Marshport, Oh." This peeled back the curtain a bit more. He found the bar had been converted into a house in the 1960s after the business shut down due to devastating fire damage. The Marshport Historical Society had declared it a historical site, which allowed the usage of town funds to renovate the building. After the conversion, it remained vacant for years before being used as a rental property.

While scrolling, he stumbled across a headline from over ten years ago: "Missing Marshport Boy Declared Runaway." A message in the comment section mentioned the Hilltop, which had thrown the article into the mix of search results. He slowly dragged the cursor over and clicked on the link.

Twelve-year-old Dillon Jackson, the missing Marshport boy, has been declared a runaway. Authorities had been searching for Dillon after his mother, Vanessa Jackson, reported him as missing over three weeks ago. Police now have reason to believe he has run away from home. The boy had recently been in communication with his father, who lives in Torwood, Ohio, and requested to move in with him after an argument with the mother. Dillon's mother had no official comment but holds out hope that he will return. After questioning, the father is not a suspect at this time.

Damon printed out the article and, once again, walked up to the front desk.

"Hey. Excuse me," he said.

The girl rolled her eyes upward in his direction without moving her head. "Ya know, man, this is normally a very quiet job. Have you ever even been in a library before?"

"Did you know him?" Damon asked, ignoring her question.

"Oh, wow. Yeah. He was in my grade, actually. He was always in trouble. I mean, it's sad what happened. But yeah."

"What happened?"

"He ran away. He had the whole town looking for him for a bit. But then once they found out he was a runaway, the whole thing kind of died off."

"No siblings?"

"I don't think so."

"It said he lived here with his mom. Do you know what happened to her?"

"I don't know. I was little. The whole thing was a big story for a minute and then . . ." She paused and thought to herself. "Then I didn't really even hear about it. I kinda forgot all about it until now." She popped up in her chair, finally showing a sign of excitement. "Oh my god. He lived in your Hilltop House."

"Hey, can you tell me anything about the little girl from that house?"

"The one who died?"

"Yeah."

"I mean, it depends on who you ask. Most people get all skittish and won't talk about it. Like if they do, they'll manifest some curse or something.

"Not you?"

"Dude, I'm going to community college and working at a library in BFE. Pretty sure I'm already cursed. But I always heard back in the day they used to do, like, experiments in the basement. Like, weird mind control and Frankenstein type stuff."

Damon waited for her to break and slip in some sarcastic remark. But she just kept looking at him.

"That so?" he finally said.

"Hey, man. You asked."

"Thanks. Umm, can I check out the Marshport books?"

"You don't have a library card."

"Can I get one?"

"Yeah, chill out. Here's the form. You can only check out three books on your first day with a card."

"You messing with me again?" he said with a chuckle.

"Why would I lie about that?"

"No, just— Never mind. I'll take these three," he said, grabbing the thickest books available.

CHAPTER TWENTY-FIVE

The lightning and thunder flashed and boomed in sync with Damon throwing open the door to the sheriff's station, scaring Gladys into an audible gasp.

"Oh my. What are you comin' in here like that for? My heart can't take that nonsense," she said.

"Is Sheriff Mason in?"

"Yes, but he's on a call,"

Damon walked past, barely acknowledging her.

"Mason!" he yelled.

He barged into the office, garnering an offended look from the sheriff. Sheriff Mason put a finger up, telling Damon to hold on.

"Yes, I do hear you Mr. Jenkins," Mason said. "And I know Jeffrey was over there last week to measure the property lines. I'm sorry you weren't happy with the results. But we checked out the whole thing, and your fence was dang near two feet into his yard. You'll have to move it. Uh-huh . . . well maybe if you wouldn't have cut down the branches to his sycamore tree that you said were on your property, he wouldn't be such a stickler for this. Okay, well we can put a pin in it and bring it up in the next town meeting. Yeah, I need to go now. Have a good one." He hung up the phone and looked up at Damon.

"You find something useful? Or you just deface some more property?"

"Dillon Jackson."

The sheriff raised his eyes and shook his head. "Is?"

"Dillon Jackson went missing in Marshport ten years ago," he said as he tossed a pile of papers on the desk.

"Oh. The runaway?"

"If you want to call it that? He was never found. I checked. The father never saw him."

"What's your point?"

He stared at the sheriff, waiting for him to catch on, but the man looked back with a blank stare. "It was from the same house! It means there's a pattern of missing children all from the same house." He forcefully gestured at the papers he'd gifted the sheriff.

"Oh, c'mon, kid. That's a stretch. Over the span of a decade, there's been a runaway, an unfortunate accident, and now the Newcommer boy. Look, I want to find him as much as you do, but you must do this right. I have been at this a long time, son. It's easy to get excited and think you found a break, because you want nothing more than to do it. But I have also seen the look on parents' faces when you have to backtrack and tell them what you thought was a sure thing was actually a dead end. You gotta be careful and cautious."

"I get that. But how did this not even pop up on your radar? I can't do my job if you don't give me all the details."

"Are you trying to insinuate something?" Sheriff Mason sat up straighter in the desk chair and locked eyes with Damon. "And what exactly is your job? Because I got half a mind to tell the Newcommers they're payin' you to spend as much time looking into anything shiny that comes along instead of trying to find their missing son. Now, I have been more than accommodating to your needs. More than I am actually required to. What I won't stand for is you barging in here and making demands and accusations. That's at least the second time you've hinted that I'm not bustin' my ass, here."

It was more a clear statement than hint, Damon thought. But he didn't push the issue. He instead relaxed his shoulders and took a seat. "Can I see the file for the Dillon Jackson missing child case? As well as any other missing child cases either closed or still open."

"Sure. Ain't much to go through. But yeah."

The sheriff reached over and slid open his top desk drawer. He pulled out a key ring and led Damon to the storage closet containing all the old case files for the town.

"This should have everything you're looking for. Sorry it's not more organized. It's one of those things that's been on the to-do list for a while now."

"Can I take—"

"Of course not," the sheriff said, as if having anticipated the question. "But you can use the interrogation room as long as it's open to spread out and unpack it all. I'd say you're pretty safe. Unless, of course, Sam Jenkins does something stupid about his neighbor's fence dispute."

"Thank you," Damon said.

"If you find anything, be sure to let us know and we will follow up on it. Together. Can't have you destroying the whole damn town cuz you found out some kid fell off their bike on Rosemary Drive fifteen years ago."

As Sheriff Mason exited, Damon moved box after box to the interrogation room. He spread out all the information for any missing child case in Marshport. Other than the ones in question, there were only a handful unaccounted for. One file contained a missing child who was quickly found and turned out to be a custody dispute violation. Another was an open-and-shut case of a child who walked home from school when they weren't supposed to. The oldest was from 1971, where Scotty Maynard made a detour on the way home to play at the park and didn't tell anyone—to the panic of his mother, Mary.

This can't be it, he thought. Even in an arguably uneventful place like this, it seemed like he was missing something. The entire criminal history of their acclaimed town stored in a few columns of carboard boxes in a closet? Damon called out to Gladys, and she appeared in the doorway.

"Yes?" she said.

"You sure this is everything? I just need to make sure. Seems like there should be more."

"Well, that's everything we have paperwork for, yes. If we can settle issues quickly, we don't bother filing reports. It's a hassle. And of course, anything we had before the fire went up as kindling along with the old bones of the station itself."

"Wait, the sheriff station burned down too?"

"Oh, yeah. There was a rash of them. Arson. Some delinquent kids. Parents were out doing drugs and whatnot and leaving them alone to run amok." She squeezed the small gold-plated cross hanging from her necklace. "Good values are just so important for kids to thrive. Otherwise, they're nothing but lost little sheep."

"Thanks, Gladys. I think I'm good."

Damon sifted through a few others before pulling back out the file for Dillon Jackson. The contact information for his mother was still listed, and he wondered if it was current. He peered out the door. Gladys was already concentrating on a word search on the back page of today's Marshport Tribune. He pulled out his phone and snapped a bunch of pictures of the files of interest before packing the boxes back up and leaving.

CHAPTER TWENTY-SIX

Damon paced back and forth in his room at the bed and breakfast. The TV offered white noise as he focused on the library books, notes, and pictures piled on the old rolltop desk against the wall. The lamp attached to the desk offered just enough light to struggle to work in the shadowy space.

In 1967, a group of arsonists had plagued Marshport. Within six days, the police station, the Hilltop Bar, the church, the jewelry store, and the butcher shop were all damaged and burned. From this, the Marshport Historical Society had been created. Their mission was to transform and rebuild around the nucleus of what made Marshport desirable to begin with.

The thunderstorm continued just outside the window, making it feel much later than five in the evening. Giant drops of rain crashed against the glass, trying to enter the room.

He flipped through his notes, trying to make sense of them. Pieces he picked from the police files, as well as notes logged from talking to the townspeople and listening in on conversations. Normally this was a big part of the job, and fairly easy to do with everyone so self-centered and unassuming of who's around them. The people of Marshport made this problematic as he continued to be spotted and asked who he was. In less than a week, he'd managed to devolve into a glowing boil in the town. He was either asked who he was based on being an outsider or immediately called out as the specific outsider looking into the town's current disappearance.

His only saving grace was the people who thrived on gossiping and oversharing. He managed to scrounge up a few leads that way. And of course, the sheriff helped, though that assistance was mostly through gritted teeth and defensive posturing. Still, Damon didn't hold it against him. It must be tough to be told your incompetence had forced the hand of reeling parents who desperately wanted their child back.

He checked his messages, mostly to clear all the little red numbers off his home screen. As he pulled it up, he wondered why voicemail was still a thing at all, and how long until it quietly went away. He blindly deleted the unknown numbers from obvious solicitors but listened to the one from his uncle.

"Damon, I'm sorry. I don't even know if you'll listen to this. But you won't message me back. Just come back and we will work everything out. I know you're on that missing child case. But take an afternoon. We need to talk. They found the money. You're not . . . not too trusting to do this. I didn't mean it. I'm sorry it got heated. I think it's just been hard. For both of us recently. I know I said you're not ready to branch off, but I was trying to pu—"

An abrupt bang shook the door. Damon jumped and fumbled his phone onto the bed.

"Hello?" he called out. He crept to the door. It was solid pine, painted blue with six white accent rectangles. There was a chain to lock, but no eye hole. No fire evacuation instructions or map to the ice machine. Simply a door hanger attached to the top to hold coats or robes.

"Hello?" he asked again, to nobody in particular. He unhooked the chain and placed his booted foot as a stopper about six inches from the opening. He pulled the door open, peering out into the dimly lit hallway.

No one stood waiting. Beyond the door was just green wallpaper patterned with pastel pink flowers and the generic wildlife paintings hanging along the empty hallway. And a single envelope sitting on the floor in the middle of the doorway. The stationary held no official letterhead or postage. He picked it up and flipped the envelope over, exposing the only marking on the white rectangle pouch.

Damon Williams

He thought it weird, but not ominous.

He had no plans to check out, so his first thought, an itemized billing receipt delivered hastily by an employee of the inn, didn't land. He opened the door the rest of the way to look down the hall. There were no other envelopes left at the door of any other rooms, though now that he thought about it, he wasn't sure if any other rooms were being occupied. Damon ventured out and wandered the halls with the letter in his hand. He looked down the interjecting hallway before turning back, passing his room, and wandering down the other way. Seeing nothing, he gave up and returned, closing and locking the door behind him.

Damon sat at the foot of the bed. Using his key as a letter opener, he cut the top of the envelope. Inside was a single piece of notebook paper with a blunt cautionary message written boldly in black Sharpie.

Stop digging. Leave immediately. You are not safe here.

He ran out and looked back and forth down the hallway again, then grabbed his keys and marched downstairs. The only person in the lobby was Sherri, who stood at the front desk as she pecked away on the computer.

"Oh, is there something I can help you with, Mr. Williams? Were you ready to grab a table for supper?"

"No, I'm fine. Thanks, Sherri. Did you leave anything at my door?"

"Oh, no. I try and avoid those stairs as much as possible.

Bad knees, ya know."

"Did you see anyone come through here?"

"Oh, a couple of guests—and we did just get the fruit delivery. It arrived late today. Luckily, we still had enough for breakfast this morning. But nothing out of the way. Why? Is there an issue, Mr. Williams?"

He started to pull the letter out from his pocket, then stopped himself and slid it back in.

"Uh . . . no. I'm good. Thanks."

Damon walked back up to his room and locked the chain once more. He slid the bedside table over to the door, knowing it wouldn't stop anyone, but at least it would make a lot of noise if someone tried to enter. He picked his phone up from the bed, still lying partially burrowed beneath the comforter.

From the picture he'd snapped of Dillon's file, he wrote down the listed number of the boy's mother.

Again, he made his rounds of the room. Looked out the window. At the pile of information on the desk. Slid the nightstand away from the door and peered out through the opening roughly eight chain links wide.

He took his seat at the foot of the bed and dialed Vanessa Jackson's number.

CHAPTER TWENTY-SEVEN

Julie stared at the phone as it rang on the table. The disdain flowed through her in icy waves as Corrine's picture bounced on the screen. She ignored it and continued cleaning the kitchen. It rang again before cutting out, and a message came through. Julie's curiosity got the best of her, and she had no choice but to see what it was.

Please call me. I have an idea. For Adam. And I need you for it.

She tossed the phone face down and stared at it. Then she slammed it repeatedly on the counter, longing to still have the ability to physically hang up on someone in anger.

Who did Corrine think she was? How did she have the audacity to try to act like she was on Julie's side? It was her fault. If she didn't have something to do with it, her negligence allowed it to happen. So, either way, she was wholly responsible. And Phillip. Fucking weirdo. He'd always kind of creeped her out. Julie couldn't believe they'd been friends with them for so long. Though to be honest, that was all Wyatt. If she had left him when she began to have doubts, and not waffled around about whether she should stay for the children, none of this would be happening. It consumed her, dwelling on all the ways she had practically begged for something terrible to happen.

Julie walked away and got halfway down the hall before stopping. She hated herself for giving in. But after screaming at the ceiling, she turned around and returned the call. It only rang once before Corrine picked up.

"Julie!"

Julie winced at the sudden high-pitched greeting and pulled the phone away from her ear.

"Yeah. You called?" Julie said, her voice a contrasting emotionless monotone.

"Yes, but the thing is, I can't really talk to you about it over the phone."

"What's going on, Corrine? I don't have time for this."

"Julie, I'm being fucking serious. Stop acting like this. I know you blame me. I get that, and I've kept my distance. But the side eyes when you're in town, the missed calls—I'm over it. I've also been trying to find him, because you know I love him and want nothing more than to get him home safe."

Julie sat silent. Different responses ran through her mind, overlapping and contrasting with each other. So, she gave none.

"Hello?" Corrine said, sounding like she wondered if she were suddenly talking to herself.

"Are you free now if I came over?" Julie asked.

"Yes. Yes. Absolutely."

***

Julie sat in the car in the middle of the O'Learys' driveway. What exactly was she getting herself into? Or, perhaps, what had she accidentally signed up to do?

She looked around the yard, finally becoming fixated on the end of the side where it met up with the woods. She wasn't quite sure what she was staring at or expecting to find, like she'd just so happen to come across Adam playing mindlessly in a tree, unaware of what a commotion he'd stirred up. Or even sprinting from the wooded area, screaming her name. "Mom! Mom! I found you! I was so scared." But nothing. Just the familiar calm that Julie had grown to loathe with every fiber of her being.

When she reached the front porch of the O'Learys' house, Julie took a moment for herself before knocking. It was the first time she'd been there since Adam's disappearance. It seemed like so long ago, but had only been roughly two weeks. Two weeks since she'd heard her baby laugh.

Before she could raise her finger to the doorbell, the door opened with a slow, drawn-out creak. Julie scanned the family room. As she walked in, she jumped at a thump from behind the door. Corrine was on the other side, picking up the shoes that had piled up.

"Sorry, I saw you walking up. I just wanted to get these out of the way. Figured I'd . . . just grab the door before you changed your mind." She chuckled nervously and trailed off as Julie stood unresponsive before her.

"What did you want to talk to me about that couldn't be discussed over the phone?"

"Can I get you anything to drink? I just got this new chai —"

"I got coffee on the way here."

"Oh. Okay. Uh, come sit down."

Julie followed her to the kitchen table and sat across from her.

"So, I have an idea, and I want you to hear me out fully before you respond. I want to bring Adam home as much as anyone. I know how it looks and why you can't even look at me. It kills me that he's missing at all, let alone that it happened from here while I was home."

The more Corrine explained herself and set up what her motives were, the more Julie regretted sitting there. She could barely breathe. This icy void of a house drained her more and more with each passing moment.

"Corrine, get to the point."

"The point is . . . I think he's still here."

"God dammit, Corrine." Julie slid back from the table and walked to the window, looking out into the back yard, as if it would somehow calm her nerves. After a second, she whipped back around. "You see? This. This is exactly the kind of—"

"No, listen, look at the facts, Jules. And then broaden your horizons. He was here. You talked to him on the phone, at like two in the morning. I checked on them before I went to bed. Phillip saw him before he left for work. You know he didn't run away. All his stuff was still here, including his phone. And no one came in or left the house."

"So what? He's been playing fucking hide and seek this whole time?" As Julie spoke, she inched forward closer to the table, but her arms remained crossed and her shoulders rose tight to her earlobes. She hovered somewhere between sitting back down and sprinting for the door.

"Not exactly. I feel like he's still here, but just not here," Corrine said, gesturing around the room.

Julie looked at the floor and shook her head. "I really don't have time for this."

"I said listen to me. Sit down. Please."

Julie looked at Corrine's sincere, pleading eyes. She mindlessly and softly bit down on the inside of her lip, before the entirety of her upper body collapsed and she sat back down in the chair. As Corrine continued, Julie heard no more trepidation or nervousness in her voice. Only hopeful determination.

"I feel him, Jules. I sense him here. Like the girl, but different. He's not gone, but like, his spirit is still here."

"Corrine, my son is missing, and I am not going to listen to your crystal-power, moon bullshit right now."

"It's not bullshit. It's science, Jules. Backed by studies. And I've been following ways to communicate with other . . .

planes. Other . . ."

"Other dimensions?" Julie deadpanned. "Like I'm going to open your fridge and have a demon dog growling at me? Get the fu—"

"Other realities. And what else happened, then? You tell me. We have nothing else. So just take a step back and ask yourself, 'What if? What if we can reach him?' I'm not certified in astral communication, yet, but I've been studying and practicing, and I think we can do it. I need you, though."

"Not certified? There's classes? Really. Oh my god, Corrine. Do you hear yourself?"

"It won't work unless you're all in. I need you to keep an open mind. And trust me."

Julie scoffed and shook her head once more. Corrine slowly reached across the table and took her friend's hands into her own. Julie recoiled and looked away, but felt a hole being stared into her until she caved and turned back toward Corrine.

"Please," Corrine said.

Julie shot up.

"No! God dammit, I don't even know why I came here. What am I even doing here?"

She rushed out the door, sliding on the sidewalk in her haste and slightly losing her footing, but she stopped and regained balance. Her phone rang. Julie slipped it out from her coat pocket and answered without bothering to look who it was, happy to have a distraction from the current situation.

"Hello," she said. She struggled to catch her breath and her temples pulsed as she immediately repeated, "Hello?"

"Uhh, Mrs. Newcommer?"

She rolled her eyes and looked at the phone screen. "Oh, Damon. Sorry. Hi. Thank you so much for calling. What can I do for you?"

"Actually," he said. "I want to know if you're open to a small road trip. I don't know if this will lead to anything, but I need to follow up on it. There's a boy who is listed as a runaway officially. But the details are too odd to ignore. I was able to locate his mother. She lives only about two hours from Marshport. I was hoping you'd come along."

"Why me?" she asked.

"Well, she was reluctant to even meet with me. So, I'm not entirely sure how this will go. And I kind of feel she'll close up unless you're with me. She'll connect with you."

Julie looked back at the house, at Corrine still standing in the doorway.

"Absolutely," she said.

CHAPTER TWENTY-EIGHT

Julie began to feel carsick as Damon swerved around the cracked and uneven parking lot of Vanessa Jackson's apartment complex. The property was sectioned off into multiple tan brick buildings, each one identical.

"There," she said, pointing to the one labeled 30-34.

When Damon parked, Julie looked out at the faint, spotty, yellow outlines of the spaces and the many patches of dirt and loose gravel. Off on the perimeter of the lot, a small playground consisting of a metal slide, rusted merry-go-round, and two swings was surrounded by a chain-link fence with a latched gate to enter.

As they walked in the entrance, a small landing led them to immediately head either upstairs or downstairs. They descended to find 32B. The hallway leading to Vanessa Jackson's apartment smelled stale and the fluorescent lighting above them buzzed and flickered.

Julie must have been projecting how nervous she was, because before Damon knocked on the front door, he cleared his throat and said, "Thanks for coming with me. I don't know what's going to come of this, but if it gets too overwhelming, just shoot me a look. You can talk as little as you want to, really."

"I just hope we can learn something," she said.

Damon knocked on the steel burgundy door. One by one, the locks and chains disengaged on the other side, and the door swung open.

"Hello," said the woman who answered. Silver streaks lined her dark hair, which accompanied heavy, tired eyes.

"Hello, Ms. Jackson. I'm Damon Willi—"

"I know who you are. We talked on the phone. You said you'd be coming alone."

"Yeah, I know but . . . well—"

"Hi. I'm Julie," she interrupted, hoping to save face with the woman who already seemed to regret meeting them. "I'm the reason we're here. My son Adam is missing."

Vanessa looked Julie up and down, then turned her gaze back to Damon.

"Come in," she said. She opened the door the rest of the way, making room for them to enter. "Close the door behind you, please."

Damon and Julie looked at each other before following and closing the door behind them as asked. Vanessa led them into the living room. A rectangular coffee table sat in the middle of a couch and two armchairs, all with the same bluish-gray microfiber material. They were all worn with age, but the chair facing the television must have been used the most regularly. The fabric on the right arm was frayed, exposing the inside where the padding was missing, like it had been plucked and picked at mindlessly over the years.

"Have a seat," said Vanessa. "I'll be right back. Can I get you anything to drink? I have water, pop, tea . . ."

"Water would be great. Thank you," Julie said.

"I'm fine. Thanks," Damon added.

As she left, Damon nudged Julie with his elbow and pointed toward the kitchen, which was in plain view. Empty liquor bottles lined the countertops, and beside the sink sat a collection of prescription pill containers.

"I think this is a mistake. Maybe we should just go," he whispered to Julie.

"No, I need to talk to her." She hadn't come all this way just to leave with nothing.

Vanessa returned soon after with a glass of water and some hot tea for herself.

"How long has he been gone?" she asked, as she slowly stirred her drink.

Damon opened his mouth to answer, but Julie beat him to it. "Almost two weeks."

"Mhm . . ." Vanessa said. "And let me guess, you don't feel any closer to getting your son back, do you? Nothing since the day it happened?"

"Ms. Jackson, it says in the report that your son ran away," Damon said.

"I'm aware of what's in the report, so if that's why you're here—"

"No, it's—" Damon paused, looking like he wanted to choose his next words carefully. "Can you tell me anything about that time? What you think happened."

Vanessa expelled a soft, thoughtful sigh. Like she hadn't decided yet if she wanted to divulge her beliefs on the subject or not. She turned to Julie. "How long have you lived there?".

"Oh, we don't. Our friends do. Adam . . . my son, was spending the night at their—"

"I'm sorry. I truly am. But I really don't know what it is you want from me," Vanessa said. "I don't have answers, and I'm not looking to start a support group."

"Vanessa, all I want is to bring my son home," Julie said. "I don't know where he is, and I'm scared, and I have to imagine he's scared too waiting for us to save him. And it can't be a coincidence that both our boys up and disappeared from there. It can't be. So, if you can think of anything that would help me, I feel maybe like we can help you, too."

"There's nothing you can do."

The bluntness of the answer threw Julie against the back of the couch. She wanted to follow up, but the words got caught in her dry, swollen throat.

Damon chimed in. "Did anything seem weird to you? Anything that stuck out? Can you remember anything from that time?"

"I remember everything from that time!" Vanessa said. "It's all I think about. There is no moving on. If there's ever a day I distract myself long enough to not feel completely guilty, I snap back and feel even worse. And you get to a point where you just . . ." She closed her eyes and rubbed her forehead. When she reached up, the sleeve of her robe slid to her elbow, exposing scars up her forearm. "You wish they'd at least find a body. Because then you'd know. It'd be over. It's the questions that eat you alive. The scenarios that play out in the mind. My son did not run away. Me and his father had our issues, but we both love him. He was a happy child. He had his problems, sure. I still, every time I open that door, imagine him standing on the other side, eager to tell me he's been fine this whole time and he's sorry for making me so worried. And we embrace and cry and he asks me to cook him some food because he's famished. And then the absolute shattering feeling that there's nothing there. Nothing on the other side of that door but stained carpet and a dim hallway. Every day for ten years, my son is taken away from me all over again. The same feeling smacks me every single day. It doesn't dull with time. There's no grief counselor if there's no one to officially grieve for."

As Vanessa spoke, Julie looked at the woman sitting in front of her and wondered who she was before; years ago, moving into a new home for a fresh start. Was this all a result of losing her child? Or was it always there? The self-abuse. The isolation. She couldn't help but wonder if Vanessa had more in common with Julie or her mother. "Ms. Jackson, I'm so, so sorry. What do you think happened to your son?" she asked.

Her nostrils flared. Her next breath filled her lungs, but she exhaled in short rapid bursts, her bottom lip quivering. "That house is evil. It took him from me. And the whole town knows it. Nobody that grew up there ever lives in it. It's always the outsiders. The people who need a leg up. They feel like they've been thrown a lifeline. Nice town. Sweet, slightly doe-eyed community. What they don't know is they're being fed straight to the devil. There's a dark cloud over that whole area hiding behind the allure of small-town charm."

"Did anyone try and help?" Damon asked.

"They put on a good show. But that's all it is. They're scared of it too. They may not fully understand, but they respect it. Don't wanna get too close. That sheriff, he acted like he cared, but as soon as he could dismiss it, he planted the seeds to cut and run from the whole thing." She blew on her tea, which couldn't possibly have still been necessary, and took a sip. "Why do you think they declared Dillon a runaway? No one looks for runaways. Oh, they'll circulate some fliers, but there's no active investigation. All real detective work stops."

"Did you know of any other children in the town who had gone missing?" Damon asked.

"In Marshport?" Vanessa said. She set her cup down on the coffee table before her and shook her head. "I was never part of their little community. It always seemed off to me. A little too . . . I don't know. Idealistic may not be the right word. But, like, too good to be true. I thought it was a small-town thing, but the town-wide church fundraisers, and the community picnics, and the themed block parties . . ."

"Did you know anything about Ava Henderson?" Damon asked.

"I don't know that name."

"She was a little girl who lived there after you. Except, she unfortunately died in the house."

"Well, that's terrible. But I don't know anything about that. I wish it surprised me."

"Vanessa—" Julie started, but was immediately cut off.

"I hope you find your son. I really do. And you hold him tight and get the fuck out of there and never look back. But, please. I can't talk about this anymore. Start to feel the walls close in around me all over again."

Julie wrapped her hands around Vanessa's and looked her in the eyes. "I understand. Thank you for your time. I know this wasn't easy for you."

The ride back into Marshport was mostly quiet, save for the hum of the tires on the highway asphalt. Julie looked out over the flat, gray, Ohio horizon in disbelief. Maybe something deeper was happening here. Maybe Corrine was right. When every logical explanation ran into a dead end, where was there to turn? After over an hour of silence, Julie turned to Damon and continued a conversation she'd been having alone in her head for much of the ride.

"Do you believe her?" she asked.

"I . . . I don't know. I believe that her son didn't run away. As far as the other stuff, well I'm still processing that."

"My kids are all I have. With everything failing around me, my career, my marriage, at least I was a good mom. Or I thought, at least." She let out a dry, airy chuckle. "I learned from the worst. I knew everything to do because it was the opposite of what my own mother did. But you know what? The most fucked up part? I always felt safe. Even after my father left us. All the nights I had to fix mac-and-cheese at ten years old for me and my little sister, while Mom was passed out on the couch. Or all the extended stays with my aunt while Mom was in rehab. Hell, my sister didn't even know the difference. She just thought we were having long sleepovers and then Mom would come back a new person. And it would be good for a bit, but always go right back. But . . . but we were never in danger. We were never scared. We always had a bed to sleep in and people who loved us——"

"Don't do that," Damon said. "That's not fair to yourself. None of this is your fault."

"Isn't it? I knew. He told me he didn't feel comfortable. If I was worth anything, my mother's intuition would have kicked in. Even when he tried to downplay it, I should have known." As she talked, she remained forward facing. She barely moved her emotionless face, except for the words that slowly spilled out of her mouth, overflowing and falling into her lap. "Mr. Williams, I don't think you're going to be able to find Adam."

CHAPTER TWENTY-NINE

Julie opened the door to Adam's bedroom and crept inside. She stood in the middle of the room and felt, even for just a moment, that she was one with him. She and Adam were together. The room was his energy, somehow a young boy and an old soul—there were action figures and video game posters, but from as early as she remembered, he'd loved so many things from before his time. Movies from the '80s and '90s. Any playlist he made mixed current music with sprinkles of Nirvana and even Elvis or the Beatles. She crawled into his bed and lay on her side with her knees tucked into her chest. She pulled his pillow into her face and inhaled. It still smelled like him. Like he had slept in it just last night and was only off to school for the day.

Julie melted into the comforter until she eventually dozed off. It was the first time she'd truly slept in over a week. She awoke to a soft knock on the bedroom door, unsure of how long she'd been out.

"Hey, there you are," Wyatt said, peeking his head in. "I took the rest of the day off today. I needed it. They're gonna dock me, but I don't care. I'm probably going to be in the garage for a while. But I'll be leaving in a bit to run some errands. Is there's anything I can do for you before I leave?"

Without response, she rolled over, turning her back to him and facing the wall. She wasn't even angry. She wanted to be angry. At least then she would feel something, anything at all other than emptiness.

She closed her eyes and listened to the floor creak against his footsteps as he walked away.

Julie pulled her phone from the front pocket of her hooded sweatshirt and called Corrine. The ringing seemed to go on forever, giving her ample opportunity to change her mind, but eventually she was greeted on the other end.

"Julie? Hey? Umm . . .I'm gonna be honest. I don't know what to say. 'What's up' seems insensitive? As does what can I do for you? I don't think you're just up for a chat. I'm sorry. I—"

"Corrine, please shut up. Can . . . I just called . . . ugh. That communication thing? You really think it will work?

"I really, really do."

"I'm in."

***

"Hey, I wasn't sure if you'd actually come," Corrine said, answering the door.

"I wasn't sure I would either, to be honest," Julie said, thinking of the multiple times on the drive she'd almost instinctively pulled a U-turn and returned home.

"No Wyatt?"

"Oh, I didn't even mention it. I was going to ask him, but he talked about running errands or something and I couldn't even get into it with him again. I didn't have it in me."

"Oh, I just figured he'd be with you since he and Phillip had to go do something after Phillip got home."

"Really?" Julie perked up. Had he mentioned that? Had he not bothered? "Wyatt didn't say anything about it, I don't think. But I guess we're not really talking all that much. Did he say what they were doing?"

"Not specifically. I can check if you want."

She shook her head. "Nah. It's fine."

As Corrine prepared the table for the ceremony, Julie uneasily passed the time by looking over the pictures on the wall she had seen a million times before. She stopped at one of the three boys playing together at their house. It was from over five years ago, and they were all in their winter gear, building snow forts. Their wind-chapped cheeks glowed red, but that didn't get in the way of the giant smiles on their faces. Adam was missing three of his front teeth at the time, making the photograph, which would normally bring a smile to Julie's face, all the more saddening.

"Have you ever done this before?" Julie asked.

"I haven't led any. But I have sat in and assisted. It's . . . it's surreal. But eye-opening."

She turned from the framed memories to Corrine. "You never told me that."

"Well, you're kinda judgy about these things."

Julie looked down at the floor and played with the zipper of her open jacket.

"Did they work?"

Corrine smiled. "Oh, yeah. I wouldn't be doing this if they hadn't. Do you have the photo and the token?"

"Oh, shit. Yes. Here," Julie said. From her purse, she pulled a five-by-seven school picture of Adam and one of his Batman action figures.

Corrine placed them between two candles at the head of the kitchen table. She closed the shades, cut off all the lights, and slowly took her place at the end.

"Come. Sit," she said, gesturing to the chair across from her.

Julie sat down as Corrine lit the candles and some incense before laying her hands palm up. Distracted by the spectacle, it took a second for Julie to notice.

"Oh," she said just above a whisper. "Sorry."

Julie took Corrine's hands, completing the circle. Between them were the candles, the incense burner, the photo of Adam, and his favorite action figure.

Corrine smiled at Julie and closed her eyes. She took a deep breath and bowed her head. Julie did her best to match the actions.

"Okay," Corrine said. "We are seated here and calling out to Adam Newcommer. We want to communicate with you. We are calling out, Adam, for you to speak with us. To come home. We need you, Adam. We miss you. Adam, it's me, Corrine. If you can hear me, give a sign."

They waited in silence briefly before she continued.

"We are seated here calling out for Adam Newcommer. Adam, if you can hear me, this is Corrine, sweetie. I know you must be scared, but I'm here with your mom, and we want you to come home. Adam, if you can hear us, give us some sort of sign."

They waited again. Julie squeezed Corrine's hand, and Corrine squeezed back.

"Adam, this is Corrine. We need you to come home. Give us a sign that you are here with us, a sign that you're okay."

When this was met with silence once more, Corrine said to Julie, "Speak out to him."

"Adam, uh . . . it's Mommy, sweetheart. I want to talk to you. Please answer me, bud. Are you with us now? We miss you and are all so worried. Your dad and your brother, too." Julie paused and smiled slightly, clearing her throat. "Your brother actually—actually got in a fight defending you. Which I know sounds so wrong to be smiling about, but . . . I can't explain it. I just want you home. I want to hold you and hear your laugh and watch Jurassic Park." She sniffed and choked out a slight chuckle. "All of them except III, of course, because I know you hate it. I want to make you pancakes and lose to you in video games. Adam, if you can hear me, give us a sign." She looked up from the table, past the ceiling, past the roof, straight into the sky. With a cracked voice, she said, "Please talk to me, Adam. Just say something. Please."

The thick, sticky silence sat heavy in the room. It hung over Julie and Corrine, smothering them. Julie sat in the frankincense-infused candlelight with any shred of hope rapidly bleeding out from her. She ricocheted from feeling hopeful, to foolish, to gutted. The longer she was met without response, the farther she sank into her chair until she doubled over into herself.

"This happens," Corrine said. "I'm sorry. I'll see what we did wrong. Maybe we need Phillip and Wyatt. They say sometimes a stronger anchor to this plane helps the process. I thought we'd be okay, but maybe we need a bigger presence." She ran her fingernails up and down Julie's back. "We'll try again."

"No, we won't," Julie said. "I can't. I need this to be over. I can't. I . . . I just can't."

CHAPTER THIRTY

Wyatt sat alone at the dining room table. Julie was right. He had been distracted. He knew it. He tried and tried to keep his mind occupied so as not to deal with the guilt of that night seeping into his brain at every moment, but naturally, it was pointless. It smothered him nonstop. He needed to do something. Julie was alone, working tirelessly to bring Adam back home, and here he was letting the fear of a restraining order keep him from searching high and low. He should have gone with her. They should have been doing this together.

He pulled out his phone and texted her.

Where'd you go?

Any luck?

He sent them in rapid-fire succession, then another.

I've been stupid. And selfish. I'm so sorry. I'm finally thinking clearly.

He popped his head into Stephen's room to check on him, before remembering Stephen was with his friends after school. Trying to have some semblance of normalcy. Good luck, Wyatt thought. Here's hoping someone can.

Wyatt hopped into his truck and began to drive. He merged onto the interstate, knowing exactly where he was headed. From day one, Kirk Jameson had given him weird vibes. And if anyone in that town knew where Adam was, he did. If Adam was anywhere.

Jesus. He couldn't even think about it. Even he was starting to question his sanity.

"People don't just vanish," he told himself. "He's out there. He's out there, and he's expecting his family to be fighting for him."

He spent the entire drive thinking about what to say. At a stoplight, he opened the glove box and pulled out his revolver, which was snapped into a leather holster. He put it into his coat pocket before shaking his head and tossing it into the middle console between the front seats. He checked his phone again. Still nothing from Julie, but he wasn't surprised.

Pulling into the diner's parking lot, he sat in his running car, mesmerized by the windshield wipers streaking against the glass, all misted by the rainy night air. The van he'd been waiting for entered the parking lot and made a three-point turn into a nearby space. Wyatt killed the engine and hopped out. He only took three steps before turning around, reaching in, and grabbing the gun from the center console. He stuffed it in the back of his jeans and pulled the back of his Carhart jacket over the handle.

Wyatt looked back and forth as he jogged across the parking lot. He checked behind him once more before climbing into the passenger seat of the O'Leary's Plumbing Service van.

Phillip checked his rear view and then the side mirror.

"No one followed you?"

"Why would someone have followed me?" Wyatt asked.

"I'm just saying."

"For fuck's sake. It's not like the border is being patrolled, watching for me."

"Yeah. I guess you're right."

Phillip shifted into drive, and before long, they sat in the driveway in front of Kirk's house. As the rain came down harder, they traded swigs from Phillip's flask to calm their nerves.

"You really think Adam's in there?"

"It's the only thing that makes sense. Is Kirk home?" Wyatt asked.

"I thought so, but his car's not here. Maybe still in the shop?"

They approached the house. Wyatt casually walked up to it, while Phillip crept a few uncomfortable steps behind him. The front yard, clearly colorfully landscaped in the warmer months, lay barren, with empty flower beds and bushes of dead branches. Wyatt knocked on the door. No lights were on that the two could see. They knocked again.

"Have you been in the house before?" Wyatt asked.

"Yeah, a few times."

"Where does he usually stay?"

"Huh?"

"When the prick is home, where does he hang out?" Wyatt said.

"He's had us over a couple times, and we've hung in the dining room off the back of the house."

"Okay, I'm going back there." Wyatt marched down the front steps and around to the back of the house. Phillip hesitated but followed shortly after, slowly at first, before speeding up to a jog to catch up.

"He's got a video doorbell," Phillip said. "All the town does."

"Right. And I'm just trying to talk to him."

"You're not even allowed to be here. I can't believe I let you talk me into this."

"What else am I supposed to do? He knows something. He has to."

They knocked again, this time on the back door, only to once more receive zero response. Wyatt knocked again, a little harder.

"I guess he's not home after all," Phillip said.

"Even better."

Wyatt pulled up on the window beside the door, and it didn't budge. He tried again, gritting his teeth and quietly grunting, thinking the old house might just need some good force to comply. But it still didn't budge, only letting off a small pop as the locked window settled under the strained pull. He cupped his hands over his forehead and attempted to peer inside. The lack of light and the soft, cold rain coming down made it almost impossible to make anything out. They walked over to the cellar door, which was closed with a chain and master lock.

"That's fucking weird, right?" Wyatt said.

"A little." Phillip pulled on the rusted lock. "I have bolt cutters in the van. But that would take this to a point there's no coming back from. I can't be a part of it. He's the guy that makes my rent, ya know."

"That's what you care about right now? Look, I have to know for sure," Wyatt said.

"Look, what if . . . what if they're right?"

"About what?"

"About, you know. It's what Corrine believes, too."

"Him just disappearing? Come the fuck on, man."

"Listen, people around town, some of them mention odd things happening from time to time. I don't really believe all that, but it's started to make me question just a little. There's just—there's nothing. What makes you think Kirk had som—"

"What the hell are you insinuating? Adam wasn't abducted by aliens, or chosen by spirits, or pulled into some alternate fucking dimension. He didn't spontaneously combust, vanish, or disappear. He was taken. My son was stolen from me. And the person who lives in this house knows something about it. Now are you going to help me or not?"

Phillip dropped his head. "Of course."

CHAPTER THIRTY-ONE

Damon marched into the Marshport Sheriff's Office and up to Gladys's desk.

"Good afternoon, Mr. Williams. What do you need today?" she asked.

"Gladys! Just send him in!" Sheriff Mason hollered from his office. He sounded annoyed and tired.

Damon knocked on the desk twice and smiled at the old woman on the way by. He let the irritated summons roll off of him. He had one thing on his mind, eating away at him, but had learned the sheriff grew abrasive when he felt someone going above him or behind his back. Damon decided he'd try to do this right.

"Sheriff," he said, with an "I'm going to ask for a favor and you're not going to like it" tone in his greeting.

"Damon Williams. We might as well get you a desk here in the office, you spend so much time here." The sheriff looked him up and down. "Or a cot even. Good Lord, son, when's the last time you slept?"

"Well, I asked if I could set up shop here day one, and you told me 'No.' Anyway, I really need to investigate the body of Ava Henderson. What is the protocol for exhuming a body in Marshport?"

The sheriff choked on his Diet Coke, and as he set the can down, it foamed over the lip, running onto his desk. As he rifled through desk drawers looking for a napkin, he said, "Now dammit, boy, what in the world do you have stuck in that head of yours now?"

"Hear me out. We talked to the mother of Dillon Jackson, and she's convinced her son didn't run away. And I believe her."

"Oh, you do, do ya? Based on one conversation?"

Damon plopped himself in the chair by Mason's desk and scooted forward until he practically hovered over it.

"If you take away the declaration of him being a runaway, and look at him as a missing child who is still out there, his case lines up very closely with Adam Newcommer. Young boy, vanished in the middle of the night . . ."

"And what does this have to do with the girl?"

Damon bounced his leg up and down. He let the answer build up pressure on the tip of his tongue before releasing his theory at the sheriff.

"Well, I believe it's all connected. She could be the key. What if . . . what if she was supposed to disappear that night too? But something happened."

Sheriff Mason pinched the bridge of his nose and closed his eyes. Damon wasn't sure if he was suppressing an aneurysm or shutting down from exhaustion.

"Mr. Williams, you keep reaching and attempting to stir up shit from the past. Meanwhile, this town is trying to heal."

"And what about the families who can't?" Damon asked. "What about Adam, who's still out there somewhere?"

Sheriff Mason leaned forward and stared Damon in his eyes, slowing his speech for emphasis.

"Son, you are delusional if you think I'm gonna allow you to dig up the body of a dead child based on a hunch and an afternoon visit with a mourning mother. You have done enough damage with your wild theories. Now, I want to find that boy just as much as you. But there's a process and protocols for a reason." He shifted his weight around and went back to filling out paperwork on his desk. The lobby phone rang, and rang again. "Dammit, Gladys, you gonna answer that?"

Damon cocked his head as he looked at Sheriff Mason, studying him.

"You're scared too, aren't you?" he asked.

"Sheriff Mason?" Gladys said. "You're gonna want to take this."

Mason picked up the phone without taking his eyes off Damon.

"This is Mason . . . Yeah . . ." He slumped and rubbed his eyes once more. "Okay I'm on my way," he said. He hung up, still staring at Damon. "That was Kirk. You know why Wyatt Newcommer would be trying to break into his house?"

Damon shook his head. "No, but I'll come with you."

Mason waved him off. "No, no. I'll handle this. You go get some sleep or something. Ya look like crap."

"I can't sleep. All I think about is Adam and getting him back home."

"Then you call up Julie and see what's going through her husband's head."

CHAPTER THIRTY-TWO

Wyatt looked down at the locked cellar door once more. The rain hit it with a pinging metallic patter. "C'mon," he said to Phillip, "let's go get your bolt cutters". As Wyatt turned and started toward the van, he came to a halt, spotting a car rolling slowly into the driveway. His first instinct, that Kirk had arrived home, caused his blood to boil on the spot. He stood close to the house, staring at the vehicle. But once the driver's door opened, he saw "Marshport Police Department" printed right on the side. He pressed himself against the siding, pulling Phillip along with him as they peered around the corner.

Sheriff Mason and Officer Hewitt exited the vehicle. Mason shined his flashlight around, inspecting the area. He flashed it onto the side of the work van before turning the light toward the woods.

"Look, we haven't done anything but try and talk to Kirk," Wyatt whispered to Phillip. "Don't act suspicious."

"Are you serious?" Phillip said. "This is suspicious. I'm done." He took a deep breath and walked out toward the front yard. "Evening, Sheriff," he called out.

"Evening, Phillip. We got a call about someone poking around Kirk's house. Can I ask what it is you're doing wandering around the man's property?

"Oh, I was just trying to talk to him. We got a leak in the kitchen, and I figured I'd talk to him about it while I was out and about. Couldn't get to him on the phone. Then he wasn't opening the door, and I tried the back. Sometimes he can't hear if he's in the dining room, you know."

"Mhm. Except Kirk is the one who called us. Said Wyatt Newcommer was pounding on his door like a madman. He sent us the recording from his front door cam." Sheriff Mason shined his flashlight directly into Phillip's chest, giving a spotlight to his entire upper body. "He must be really concerned with that leak. Where is Mr. Newcommer?"

Wyatt winced and whispered "fuck" before walking up beside Phillip.

"I'm right here, Sheriff."

"Mr. Newcommer, you're not supposed to be here. I know you're aware of that."

"Yeah, I know. I—"

"I need you both to put your hands behind your backs, and get down on the ground."

"What? What did we do?" Phillip asked.

"Now," Sheriff Mason said.

Slowly, and reluctantly, they complied. He and Hewitt patted them down, and the officer pulled the gun from the back of Wyatt's waistband.

"You have a concealed carry for this?" she asked.

"Mr. Newcommer, you are in a world of problems," Mason said before he could respond. "You are at a home you're supposed to be five hundred feet from, with a firearm. You are on video being belligerent and trying to break into a man's house. Does that about sum it up?"

Wyatt deflated and sank his head as low as he could. Unfortunately, that was answer enough.

"Phillip, we have probable cause to search your van. Is there anything in there we might not want to find?"

"It's just my work van," he said.

Wyatt didn't look toward his friend, but he could tell Phillip was glaring at him from where he lay in the wet grass on his stomach.

***

Wyatt and Phillip sat handcuffed in the back of the police cruiser while the officers searched Phillip's van. Wyatt looked over to his friend, who glared down at his feet and hadn't said a word since the two were restrained. Wyatt began to say something, but nothing felt right. He felt this was just a minor set-back, but knew Phillip wanted no part of hearing him talk about that right now. Instead, he turned and silently stared out the window, observing the officers.

Sheriff Mason popped open the back hatch doors, immediately falling out of view. Officer Hewitt looked in the front, starting with the passenger side, pulling open the glove box and sun-visor. After a few minutes, Mason reeled backward from the rear double doors with his hand over his mouth. He waved Hewitt over, and they conversed briefly and inaudibly before looking back at the squad car.

Wyatt shot up, trying best he could to see anything, but he couldn't. He shot a glance to Phillip, who still slumped with his eyes fixed on the floor. When Wyatt turned back to the officers, Sheriff Mason was already approaching. He opened Wyatt's door and offered a hand.

"Mr. Newcommer, can you follow me, please?"

Still restrained and with the sheriff's hand around his arm, Wyatt was guided to the rear of the utility van. Balled up in the back, and tucked in the corner, was a child's T-shirt. A red shirt with Spider-Man on it. He hung upside down in the classic pose, except the bottom of the shirt had been ripped and tattered, leaving a portion of Spider-Man's head missing. Along the rip, and spotted across the front, was what appeared to be crusty chunks of dried blood.

Wyatt's knees buckled, and he collapsed to the ground. The sheriff swooped in and caught him, lifting him back up.

"Mr. Newcommer, I need to ask. Do you recognize this shirt?"

"That . . . that's Adam's. That's Adam's shirt." Wyatt looked over to Phillip, and then again to the back of the van. "That's Adam's shirt," he said again, this time with fire in his voice. "That motherfucker. Where is he! What happened?" he shouted back toward Phillip. "Where's my son? Where's Adam?"

Phillip's eyes grew wide.

"Mr. Newcommer, I need you to settle down," the sheriff said. "I can only imagine what's going through your head right now. But—"

"I'll kill you!"

Wyatt started to charge, his hands still cuffed behind him, but the officers caught him. He kicked and flailed but went nowhere. The officers collected the shirt in a gallon-sized Ziplock bag and called a tow truck for the van.

"I didn't do anything!" Phillip called out from the car. "I have no idea how that got in there! Wyatt, I swear. I wouldn't do that. I loved Adam! Like my own son!"

"What do you mean, you loved him?" Officer Hewitt asked. "Like in the past tense. What are you trying to say?"

"No, Jesus. Nothing like that. Wyatt, you have to believe me. There's got to be some explanation."

Wyatt sat under the overhang on the front steps of Kirk's house. His shoulders and wrists were on fire from being restrained. Beads of rain dripped off his bangs, still wet from walking around the house, and ran into his eye. He thrashed his head from side to side and exploded once more toward Phillip.

"Is that why you didn't want me to confront Kirk?" he asked. "Is that why you wanted to tell me he really did just disappear? Where is he?" His voice broke. "Is . . . is my son alive?"

"Wyatt, listen to me," Phillip said.

"Phillip O'Leary, you have the right to remain silent," Sheriff Mason said, stepping toward the car and snuffing out whatever Phillip was going to say next. He finished giving the rest of the Miranda rights and slammed the door.

Kirk arrived home and ejected himself from his car. He immediately began waving his arms around and hollering upon seeing Wyatt sitting on his front porch.

"Why is he sitting on my steps?" Kirk said. "I want him taken away this instant. Get him out of here before he snaps."

"Now, Kirk," Mason said, "I need you to go inside. May come as a shock, given the spectacle here, but this doesn't actually concern you any longer. We'll be out of your hair in just a second." He approached Wyatt. "Mr. Newcommer, I express my deepest sympathies for what is going on. Now, he hasn't spoken, but we will find out what happened to your son. We'll get it out of him. Obviously, given the circumstances, we're gonna pretend you weren't at Kirk's front door violating that restraining order tonight."

When Officer Daniels arrived to assist Hewitt and finish up, Sheriff Mason removed the handcuffs from Wyatt and helped him into the spare police car.

"Come on, I'll drive you to your truck, and then we can head back to the station."

As they pulled away from the scene, Wyatt finally lifted his head from his chest to get a last look at Kirk's front yard. The lights of the remaining police car splashed red and blue across the house and the O'Leary Plumbing van, which was being winched onto the tow truck.

"It doesn't make sense," Wyatt said, sobbing. "I've known him since college. Why would he do this?"

"Well, Wyatt, I've been in this line of work a long time. Unfortunately, it's usually the closest to us when these things happen. Which, sadly, is more often than anyone wants to admit. Like I said, we will find your son. We will press him. I'm just glad we're finally getting close."

As they pulled up to the four-way stoplight, Sheriff Mason popped the lid off his thermos, which doubled as a small mug, and poured Wyatt some coffee.

"Here," he said. "Sip some of this. It's bitter, but will help warm you up from sitting out in that rain."

"I can't believe it. This just doesn't feel real," Wyatt said, slowly sipping, and then repeated, "It doesn't make sense."

"I've been at this a long time, Wyatt. These things never do."

CHAPTER THIRTY-THREE

Wyatt, where are you? Julie texted. It was the latest of
several unanswered messages she'd sent him. *Damon said you
were seen at Kirk's house. Should I be worried?*

She heard the front door open and perked up.

"Wyatt?" she called out.

Stephen entered the kitchen wearing his winter coat with a
bookbag in tow. She eased back into her prior slumped
position.

"Oh, hey bud. How was Ross's?" she said. She tried her
best to sound mundanely conversational, to hide the worry
and concern feasting on her.

"It was fine," he said.

"H-how are you doing? I know we've all been preoccupied.
I'm sorry."

"It's fine, Mom. I get it. Where's Dad?"

"He said he had to run some errands. I'm not sure when
he'll be back. So, for now, it's just us tonight. You want
chicken strips or frozen pizza? I don't have the energy to cook
anything."

"It's fine. I already ate," Stephen said.

He grabbed a Coke from the fridge and headed down the
hall toward the stairs. He stopped with one foot on the bottom

step and turned around. Julie scanned over the counter, wondering what he could have forgotten, but he approached her and wrapped his arms around her, squeezing tightly. As she began to sob, she slid her arms up and around her son, holding him tighter.

"I love you," Stephen said.

"I love you too. So, so much," Julie said.

Her phone buzzed. Stephen tried to let her go so she could check it, but she pulled him back in. Her phone buzzed again. And again. She kissed his cheek, burying her face into the side of his, leaving it wet from the tears that rolled down and collected in the corners of her mouth. She picked up the phone to a burst of messages from Corrine.

I don't know what's happening.

Call me please.

I need you to call me.

She'd barely skimmed over the messages before "Marshport Police Department" popped up and danced across her screen. She answered, and as Sheriff Mason filled her in on what had transpired at Kirk's, she began to shake. The conversation was short and to the point, but toward the end the sheriff's voice trailed off and all Julie could hear was the high-pitched whirring inside her own head. She didn't even remember hanging up the phone. She simply set it back down on the counter and stared off into the corner of the room with her mouth agape.

"Mom, what is going on?" Stephen asked.

"They took Phillip in for the disappearance of Adam."

"What?"

"They found his—" she began to answer, but the words clogged in her throat. "They found his shirt in Philip's van."

"What? But what about Adam?"

She broke. Her eyes spilled over as she grasped for breath. "They still don't know. He hasn't said anything. I need to go. Lock the door and—"

"Mom, let me co—"

"No, I need you to stay here. I'll keep you posted on everything. I swear." She hugged him once more, grabbed her coat, and fled out the door.

***

Julie arrived at the station and barely brought the car to a stop before jumping out and storming through the doors. She approached the desk, trying to compose herself, but then she saw Phillip in the interrogation room. His head down. His hands cuffed to the table. His sullen body not emoting or giving off any energy at all. She felt the fire and hatred start pulsing through her all over again.

"Julie, there's been some kind of mistake," Corrine said. Julie whipped around.

"Don't," she said. "Don't you fucking dare. And you guys . . . ugh, he was helping Wyatt try and find him. And this whole time. Did you know? Where is Adam? Is—is he . . . ?"

"Julie, listen to me. Phillip wouldn't do this. There's been some mistake."

"Bullshit! What? You're gonna tell me the evil house swallowed him whole? You let me believe you could feel him in the house. Were you just stringing me along? Feeding me shit? For what?"

Sheriff Mason stepped between them.

"Mrs. Newcommer, I said you didn't have to come down here. I'm not gonna tell you how to handle what's going on right now, but I do need you to not scream here in my reception area. That is not conducive to anything. He hasn't talked at all yet, but he's been stewing in there all alone for a bit now, and I was gonna go and try and question him again."

"Sorry. I need to stay. I need to know."

Damon entered the sheriff's station and looked around. He walked up to Julie.

Sheriff Mason, with his hand on the doorknob to the interrogation room, looked over at Damon and sighed.

"Mr. Williams, great, you're here." He shook his head. "More people crammed in this tiny station to complicate things. Just what we need." He entered the room to join Phillip and shut the door behind him.

Julie looked to Damon. He rolled his eyes at the sheriff and turned her way.

"Hey. Anything yet?" he asked.

"No," Julie said. She sat down and covered her face with her hands.

"Where's Wyatt?"

She threw her arms up, then dropped them back down into her lap. "I have no idea. I can't get a hold of him. Stephen hasn't heard from him. He's still not home."

"Shh, shh. Don't focus on that now. We're getting close. Hewitt and Daniels are searching Phillip's work van."

"I'm telling you, there must be some mistake," Corrine said again, pleading with the others in the room. "Some explanation."

"Corrine, shut up!" Julie yelled. "You don't get to talk unless you're telling me where Adam is."

Gladys answered the ringing desk phone and held her finger up to her open ear, blocking out the noise. After a few seconds, she walked over to the door of the interrogation room and knocked rapidly and repeatedly, waving Sheriff Mason over to her. He trudged his way behind the reception desk, and shook his head at the scene. Julie knew what he was thinking, but she paid him no mind.

The sheriff pinched his eyes and hung up the phone.

"Mrs. Newcommer," he said.

She ignored him. "Why are you even here?" she growled at Corrine. "The fact you still have zero fucking problem leaving your own child tells me everything."

"Mrs. Newcommer," the sheriff said again, holding his

palm out, demanding attention.

She looked at him, then back to Corrine, who stood silently before her, appearing shattered and confused.

Sheriff Mason cleared his throat. "Julie!"

"What? I don't want to hear another word until that fucking monster tells me where my son is."

"We just got a call," he said. "A body was found in the woods tonight. Now I need you to sit—"

"Oh my god! Is it . . ." She couldn't bring herself to finish the thought aloud.

"It's Wyatt."

CHAPTER THIRTY-FOUR

Wyatt Newcommer was still hanging from the tree when they arrived.

Mason removed his hat and wiped his brow. The violence. The spectacle. His town wasn't normally in such a bad way. He prided himself on the peaceful slice of life Marshport enjoyed. But missing children? Assaults? Multiple times this week there'd been the need for lights and sirens scaring the community. And now, here he stood looking at a dead man dangling by his neck. He knew he had to close this missing child case soon. For the good of the town.

The Marshport man who'd stumbled upon Wyatt during a late-night walk with his dog stood by, waiting to give a statement. Mason stepped aside to make room for Officer Daniels to pass by him with the ladder. He propped it against the base of the tree as Mason approached and followed up with the witness.

"Sam, thanks for hanging out," the sheriff said. "I'm sure this wasn't how you planned to spend your evening. Anything you can add that may have stood out to you?"

"Well, I have been walking Luna at night ever since I saw on Facebook that late-night runs were good for the joints. Both hers and mine, probably," he said.

"And do you walk this path every night?"

"Well yeah, for about the last few months. I thought everybody knew that. I reckon I only got another few weeks before it gets too cold. But at first, I thought it was a spirit or something, the way Luna freaked. About yanked my shoulder out. But then I saw him just hanging there. Called you immediately."

"Thanks, Sam. If I need anything else, I'll reach out. Try and have a decent rest of the night."

"You too, Sheriff."

Mason glanced up at Daniels climbing the rungs of the ladder and clicked his tongue against his teeth. "Oh, it's gonna be a long one for me."

Officer Daniels cut the rope and carefully lowered Wyatt. He was confirmed dead, placed into the black vinyl bag, and sealed inside with a zip.

Sheriff Mason looked to the sky. A silver lining, if there was one, was that it had stopped raining and now clear enough to view the night sky through the treetops. "Why?" he said, looking at the stars. He reached into his inside coat pocket and pulled out a pack of cigarettes. As he lit one up, a twig snapped behind him, and he looked back to see Damon slowly approaching. The private investigator appeared visibly distraught as he got closer to the scene.

Damon struggled to soak in what laid before him. He opened his mouth, like he was about to say something, but then closed it. After staring at the medical examiners finishing up, Damon eventually said, "I didn't realize you smoked,"

"Well, if my wife asks, I don't," the sheriff said.

"Fair enough. What happened?"

"I took him to his truck after we arrested Philip. He was supposed to head back to the station with us. Never showed. He was shaken, understandably. God, I should have taken him to the station myself. Shouldn't have left him alone. If I'd have known . . . I don't know. I didn't think he was a risk like this."

"How's Julie?" Damon asked.

"Really? How ya think? I got the poor woman a room at the Stepford for now."

"You left her alone?"

Mason scoffed. "Of course not. Hewitt is sitting with her. Believe it or not, I know what I'm doing here." He took another long drag to finish off his smoke. "You took your sweet time getting out here."

"I was looking into something. We still need to find Adam. That's what I'm still focused on."

"Well, I'm sorry my attention was commandeered a bit given the circumstances."

They paused and stood by quietly as Wyatt was carted out. Damon pulled his knit cap from his pocket and slid it over his head. He blew into his hands and rubbed them together.

The sheriff chuckled at him. "It don't get cold out in Cleveland?"

He expected some kind of cutting retort, but the lack of any reaction left Mason to shake his head and study the man instead. Damon's eyes bounced back and forth between the fatal tree branch and the bag containing Wyatt's still body. The sheriff could tell the wheels were grinding inside that annoying little head of his.

"What is it, Damon?" he asked, already knowing the answer would irritate him.

"It doesn't make sense, though. It can't be a coincidence, can it?" Damon said.

"What's that?"

"The children. The pattern. It's all too similar."

He knew it. If he were a gambling man, he'd be a rich one.

"Oh jeez, kid. That again? I'm telling ya. If you look hard enough to find a common line between any two cases, you're sure to find it. You gotta look at what's in front of us. Not mold the facts to fit your decisions."

"I guess. But why now? They've known each other for years."

"I don't try and make logical sense of twisted criminal activity. It obviously wrecked Wyatt. The guilt of it all."

"But, like, what if both are true? What if he did it, but he's also not lying?"

"Kid, you're gonna give me a migraine. Don't overcomplicate it. We got Phillip for the disappearance. He's still not answering, but we can officially charge him based on the evidence and lack of a concrete alibi. Real, tangible stuff that you can see and feel. Not whatever wild scenario you got cookin' up in that brain. Now, there's nothing for you to do here. Why don't you head back to the Stepford."

"I can't right now. Check this out," Damon said quickly, like he'd been waiting for his opening. "Let me know what you think. We may not need Phillip to talk to find Adam. We know he arrived at the job site that morning on time. And we know when he left the house that morning based on the security alarm." Damon pulled out and unfolded a printed Google map with lines and circles he'd scribbled on using different colored markers. "Because it would be irresponsible to ignore what's right in front of us, here are all the paths he could have possibly taken that morning based on where he was headed." He pointed to his marked spots between the O'Leary home and the school. "And here are all the out-of-operation warehouses and storage facilities along the way. He had to stay close to the interstate based on what time he met with the principal that morning. Which means there's a good chance Adam is in one of these buildings. Real and tangible."

"You did this all that quickly?" the sheriff asked.

"Yeah."

"That's . . . well, that's great work, Williams," Mason said, genuinely impressed.

"Thanks," he said. "I'm heading that way now. I just had to see this for myself first. I still can't believe it. Did you want to come with me?"

"I need to drive Mrs. Newcommer home. But I can send Hewitt or Daniels with you."

Damon folded the paper back up and slipped it into his coat pocket.

"Yeah, if we could split this up and cover more ground, we stand a better chance. I do have to make a stop first. I still think I can streamline this more to speed up the process."

"Sounds like a plan. I'll tell Officer Hewitt when I go pick up Julie."

CHAPTER THIRTY-FIVE

Inside a spare room of the Stepford Bed and Breakfast, Julie spiraled, struggling to make sense of the night. She grasped at thread after thread, trying to weave a semblance of rational thought.

Just a couple hours prior, she was convinced of being closer than ever to having her son back. But as she sat, isolated and empty, it was like that first day all of again. Was she being punished? She couldn't help but think about Carol pleading for her to stay away. But how could she? How could anyone? And even still, it didn't make sense. Wyatt was the one who kept reprimanding her to push on despite everything. Why would he take his own life now? Her husband was a lot of things, but cowardly wasn't one of them.

Officer Hewitt sat with her inside the room, close by in a rolling desk chair. Partly to offer emotional support. Partly, Julie knew, to make she didn't do anything irrational.

She tried to call Stephen, but as she scrolled for his name, her phone flashed the battery sign and shut down. She stared at the black screen, and her own reflection looking back at her. She swallowed down whatever attempted to boil to the surface and turned to the officer.

"Do you have a phone charger?" she asked softly.

"No, I'm sorry. I can check with the desk."

She sighed. "No, don't worry about it."

In the background, the TV played syndicated episodes of The Big Bang Theory. Hewitt was mostly focused on that. She hadn't said much to Julie other than making sure she was comfortable and asking who could be called to stay with her. Which was fine. She appreciated it, and she didn't want to be alone. But she also didn't want to be here. She just wanted to be home. Home with Stephen, who still had no clue he'd lost his father. She wanted to squeeze Wyatt and Adam. She wanted to murder Phillip and Corrine. All at once, these feelings suffocated her. Wrapping over her face and neck and chest, constricting until her eyes bulged from her skull and her ribs ached under the weight.

The sheriff tapped on the doorframe.

"Hey," he said. "Hewitt, I'm gonna take Mrs. Newcomer home. Phillip is fine in the holding cell. He knows something, but he's completely shut down. He's good to rot there till morning as far as I'm concerned. I need you to get with Damon. He's got his senses on something and needs your help."

"Sound's good, Sheriff," Officer Hewitt said.

***

As Sheriff Mason pulled out of the parking lot of the Stepford Bed and Breakfast, he struggled about what to say to Julie. No combination of words existed that would make right what had transpired, and he wasn't fooling himself into thinking any sort of consoling remarks would hit the way they needed to. He felt for her, but he also was careful not to mention anything to her about Damon heading out to search for her son. And he deeply hoped the private investigator hadn't done so either. As much as she needed hope, him coming up empty handed would surely drop the bottom out from beneath her. So the sheriff decided to say nothing, other than ask for her address.

He weaved his way through the Marshport side streets, heading toward the interstate. As he drove past Kirk's house, he slowed to a crawl. Damon's car was in the driveway. He looked in the rearview, backed up slightly, and pulled in behind him.

"I apologize for this," Sheriff Mason said. "It will only take a second."

She remained silent, only responding by looking his way, then back down to her feet.

As the sheriff climbed the wooden porch steps and approached the door, he heard the two engaged in some sort of heated conversation.

"I can't with this guy," he muttered to himself. He put his hand on the cold metal door knob and braced himself before walking in.

CHAPTER THIRTY-SIX

Damon knocked on the front door of Kirk's small ranch house. It was close to eleven at night, and the curtains were drawn, but the lights shone through the border, creating a bright outline to let Damon know Kirk was still awake.

He bounced and rocked in attempt to force the universe into speeding up the man. He had to be on the road, but hopefully fifteen minutes here would save him hours tonight. As he waited, he stood staring down at the brown welcome mat with big, bold, script-like font stating "We Are Covered," and centered below it, "Psalms 91."

"Can I help you?" Kirk said, slowly opening the door, his voice cracked and tired.

"Hi, Kirk. Can I come in?"

Kirk looked at his watch. "Do you know what time it is? I was just about to wash up and head off to bed."

"I know it's late. This won't take long. Please. I need your help."

Kirk let out an exasperated sigh and moved aside for Damon to enter. "What can I help you with?"

"I'm following up on a couple of things, trying to map out a plan. I'm sure you heard by now they picked up Phillip O'Leary for the disappearance of Adam?"

"Yes, I was here when it happened. It's so sad, but I'm happy he'll be brought to justice. Did they find the boy?"

As they talked, Kirk meandered around the kitchen and living room, picking up and getting ready to pack in for the night. Damon followed closely behind him.

"No. They're questioning Phillip now, but he isn't talking. Now, he's waiting for his lawyer."

"Mhm . . ."

"I don't know, but for the first time since the disappearance, there's hope. That's actually why I'm here. To see if you can help narrow this down for me."

"Oh?"

"Yeah, I know you were with the O'Learys and the Newcommers both that evening. I was wondering if you noticed anything off with Phillip or even Corrine."

Kirk stopped wiping down the kitchen. He stood up straight and scratched his chin as he thought. "No. Not particularly."

"Did he mention anything about his commute for the next morning? Any additional stops or which way he prefers to drive?"

Kirk chuckled to himself. "I know he's frugal. Always worried about me raising the rent." He perked up like he was actually on to something. "So maybe he'd avoid toll roads?"

"Great! See, that helps," Damon said. He pulled out his folded map of scribbles and took a red marker to the turnpike. He couldn't totally rule it out, but it was enough to focus on the other areas. He looked back up to Kirk, who had already returned to cleaning and was mostly ignoring Damon. "Kirk, I have to say, you don't seem as surprised as I'd have thought, given what's happened."

"I'm relieved more than anything, Mr. Williams. Concerned, but relieved. I understand full well I have been a suspect. Given the optics, I'm just blessed to have the truth now. All of us have been tried by these recent events. I've been consciously keeping to myself because of it as much as possible. But yes, I am shaken. They seemed like good people. But I guess that's the thing, huh?"

Damon's need to dig got the best of him, and he took it upon himself to have a seat on a bar stool at the kitchen island. He thought for a second, then pulled out his notepad. As he spoke, he flipped through the notes of his investigation so far.

"How well do you know them?" he asked.

"Well, they've been my tenants for, oh, a little over two years now."

"They lived in a different property of yours, correct? Still here in Marshport?"

"Well, yes."

"It seems odd they'd need a bigger house, just being the three of them. Ya know? Didn't you find it strange?"

"Well, yes, it had been vacant since, well, you know." Kirk perked up and put his hands out in defensive emphasis. "And listen, I disclosed all of that to the O'Learys before they moved in. That's a terrible thing that happened, and I didn't want to have them find out after the fact. I know how this town loves to gossip. That's not how I do business."

"Oh, of course. I get that. That's not why I'm here."

Kirk rubbed his temples and sighed loud enough that Damon understood he was growing tired of the conversation. "Then why are you still here, Mr. Williams?"

Damon slipped his notepad and the map into the inside pocket of his jacket and zipped it back up. He rubbed his sweaty palms back and forth on his jeans. "Kirk, I've got a couple questions that are more just general. Off the record, I guess. If there really is such a thing nowadays. Because I'm not sure where they're going or even that I believe them. But" —he nervously cleared his throat— "have you ever noticed anything in that house that you can't explain?"

"Oh, I don't know. I feel like there's an explanation for everything."

"You're aware of the house's reputation, though. Correct? How some people around town say it's evil."

Kirk chuckled. "Why yes, of course. I've come to learn that when people don't have a path to follow, they'll often latch on to any superstition or wild theory as a life preserver. But houses can't be evil, Mr. Williams," he said dismissively. "Why do you have so many questions anyway?" He turned from Damon and began moving clean dishes from the strainer to the cupboard.

"Because there's still a child missing," Damon said, slamming his fist down on the countertop.

Kirk jumped at the outburst and dropped a glass, which shattered on the fake tile of the kitchen floor. "Look what you made me do," he said. "Then why are you still wasting time with me when you should be searching? Or go question Phillip some more. They found the boy's Spider-Man shirt in his van, for heaven's sake. He is the only one who knows for sure."

Damon cocked his head and stared at Kirk as he grabbed a broom and dustpan from the wall hanger. He studied the man to the point that when Kirk turned back around to sweep up the mess, he skidded to a stop upon seeing Damon's face.

"How did you know that?" Damon asked.

"Know what?" Kirk said. He still had an irritated tone in his voice Damon didn't like.

"The T-shirt," he said. "That wasn't disclosed. And the sheriff said you didn't get home until after Phillip was arrested."

"Oh, it must have gone through the gossip channels. You know how this town is by now."

"No, I've been with the sheriff's department the entire time before coming here. What they found wasn't released, let alone that specific."

"Then I must have seen them carrying it. It was right out front here. Remember?" As Kirk spoke, he didn't sweep up the glass but instead waved the cleaning supplies around in emphasis.

"Kirk, I'm going to ask you again. How do you know they found Adam's shirt in his van?"

Kirk dropped what was in his hands and began to pace, kneading away at the back of his neck.

"Kirk, how—"

"I messed up! Again," he blurted out.

The words collided into Damon's chest, and he gripped the sides of the barstool to keep from falling off. He watched as Kirk paced back and forth, bouncing off the wall, then the counter, then the refrigerator, muttering under his breath. Damon jabbed himself in the thigh with his pen to make sure he hadn't fallen asleep on the job. That he wasn't really in his car upside down on the side of the road somewhere.

"Kirk, do you know where Adam is?" he asked.

"It wasn't even supposed to be him. It was supposed to be the O'Leary boy. He could have just disappeared. I screwed it all up. Now I am being punished."

"What?"

"It's all ruined. It was not supposed to be like this." He looked up at Damon with eyes filled with regret and acceptance. "But you can't stop it. They won't let you." Kirk walked past Damon and sat down at the kitchen table. He began to sob as he talked, half directed at Damon, but half what appeared to be into the atmosphere. "It's too late. But . . . but the children don't feel pain. They never feel pain. You must know that. I make sure of it."

Damon, attempting as best he could to keep his head on straight, slowly drew his pistol from his belt and some zip ties from his jacket pocket. "Kirk, you're going to sit there, and I'm going to restrain you. Do not move. We'll wait for—"

The front door opened behind them, and someone approached slowly. "Kirk? Damon? What's going on?" It was Sheriff Mason's voice.

"Sheriff, thank god. We are arresting Kirk for connection to the disappearance of Adam Newcommer."

The sheriff winced and aggressively scratched the top of his head. His face told Damon he didn't believe what was right in front of him.

"Dammit. Phillip is detained at the station right now," he said. "What the hell are you doing?"

"He said—"

The sheriff shut the front door and locked the deadbolt.

"I was speaking to Kirk, Mr. Williams. Kirk, I am growing more and more tired of cleaning up your messes."

CHAPTER THIRTY-SEVEN

It took a moment for Damon's train of thought to catch up with what he heard from the mouth of the sheriff. He stood there for a moment, still waiting for Sheriff Mason's assistance, before the words swooped in and shattered him. He staggered backward.

The sheriff let out a long, frustrated sigh and pulled out his phone. He tapped the screen a few times before putting it up to his ear.

"Good evening . . . Yeah. I'm aware, but do you think I'd call you this late for no reason? You're out of time . . . Well, make it work. It's gotta happen now." He looked at Kirk. "Well, the whole thing just went south . . . Yep, we sure are." He put the phone away and massaged his forehead with his thumb and index finger.

Damon stared at Mason, who appeared deep in thought. In fragmented chunks, he rapidly played back every conversation and run-in the two had had. Every jagged bit of information missed. Every side-eye he'd ignored.

"Sheriff, what the hell is this?" he asked.

The other two talked, disregarding Damon.

"How was I supposed to know?" Kirk said.

"You're getting sloppy. I told 'em to retire you after you

screwed up the last time. But no."

"Just because I grieve and try to convert them does not mean I have second thoughts," Kirk said. "It's worked before. It's what we're supposed to do. Offer salvation."

"Kirk, no one is trying to say that. But look around us. All the unnecessary deaths due to your recklessness."

"I need you to tell me what the fuck is going on!" Damon said. He raised his pistol and swayed the aim between the two men, unsure who the bigger threat truly was. "What have you done with Adam?"

"Don't move a muscle, son," the sheriff said, sounding sincere yet condescending. "You're only gonna do something you regret."

"No. It's over. Take me to Adam. Now."

"Or else, what? You gonna shoot me? Really? C'mon, Damon. You're smarter than that. What would that get you?" His hands were raised, but not to surrender. They floated out in front, palms out. As he spoke, the words became softer, and slower. "You ever shot anyone before? It's not like the movies. It stays with you. Every time you close your eyes. Trust me."

Damon remained locked on Sheriff Mason, both hands gripping the pistol. Whatever this was, he wasn't buying it. His swayed aim and his shaky hands steadied into a fixed and unyielding stance. He wasn't just determined. The betrayal and humiliation fueled him as it sank in that every time he'd gotten closer to the truth, there'd been one person making him appear crazy and out of line.

"Get down on the ground, and put your hands behind your back," he said.

"I'm not gonna do that, son." The sheriff's confident swagger all but melted away, and it felt like for the first time, he talked to Damon like a human being and not an obstacle. "But I can promise you, this is the absolute worst part of my job."

"You're right, Sheriff," Kirk said.

"What're you talking about, Kirk?" he asked without looking back at him.

"Me being reckless. I can feel it. I'm no longer chosen."

"Kirk, listen. We'll—"

"I'm a detriment to the cause. To the whole town. He is punishing me. You have to offer me, as well. It's the only way back."

"Now, Kirk, will you settle down and not be so dramatic? I'm handling it, but we're kinda in the middle of something here," Mason said.

"No, you were right. I used to feel his love flow through me. His light. The mission would guide me. I'm no longer chosen."

Kirk walked closer to Damon, who took two steps back. Damon moved the gun away from the sheriff and toward the man approaching him. But the way he walked, almost floating with his hands behind his back and his forehead out, wasn't menacing. More sacrificial. Damon warned Kirk to stop, but he kept advancing until the barrel of the gun was firmly planted between his eyes. Eyes that watered and peered up at Damon with deep and clear pleading.

"You need to offer me to him, Mr. Williams. It's why you came here tonight. He sent you. I know that now."

Damon couldn't get any words out. Nothing that made sense of this situation. He tried to keep his attention on the sheriff but couldn't.

"Kirk, we'll get through this," Mason said. "We always do."

Kirk trembled as he pushed into the gun slightly harder. "Please. It needs to happen,"

Damon lowered the weapon from Kirk, who expelled a stuttered, defeated sigh and backed away until he hit the kitchen island. It didn't feel right. Damon wasn't sure if it was the way Kirk begged, or if Sheriff Mason had somehow slithered into his conscious thought once again. But he couldn't do it. Even with the facts clearly laid out before him.

"If you won't deliver me, I'll do it," Kirk said. "To make it right. To be blessed again." He reached over and grabbed the black handle of a steak knife from a wooden butcher block on the counter.

"Now, Kirk, hold on," Sheriff Mason said.

"In his name," he said.

In one fluid motion, Kirk ripped the knife from its slot and dug it into his neck, just below his ear. The serrated teeth sunk in and he dragged it across his body, tearing the flesh as he pulled. The blood spilled down the front of his throat.

Damon stood frozen. Stuck in suspended animation, wanting to simultaneously run for help, rush in to aid the man himself, and watch him bleed out the way he deserved.

Kirk's hand, wet and red, dropped the knife and it hit the linoleum in a metallic ping as his body collapsed and slid down the kitchen island. Sheriff Mason dashed forward to catch him.

"No, no, no!" he yelled, ripping off his coat and using it to apply pressure on the wound.

Kirk coughed out a wet gurgle and twitched before falling completely unresponsive. Sheriff Mason stood up and draped the now blood-soaked jacket over Kirk's limp body, offering a shroud to the gruesome display.

The sheriff hung his head. "Dammit, Kirk, it wasn't supposed to go like this. We could have gotten through it." He turned to the private investigator, then shook his head and looked back down at Kirk. "Damon, you sure have made a huge mess of everything."

As the sheriff had his moment with Kirk, Damon crept forward and put the gun to the back of Mason's head.

"It's over," he said. "Take me to Adam. Is he still alive?"

The sheriff nodded. He interlocked his hands behind his head and stood up. Damon took a half step back to keep distance between them. "We should get Julie," Mason said, turning around.

"No. Stop stalling. Turn back around," he said. He held tight to the gun with one hand as he reached for restraints with the other.

"She's in the squad car. In the driveway."

Damon paused and studied the sheriff, who didn't twitch or shuffle or look uneasy at all. His calmness in the silent house was almost unsettling. "What's she doing in there? What have you done to her?"

"She's fine, son. I was in the process of driving her home."

Damon couldn't tell if Sheriff Mason was being truthful or not. He wasn't sure what was real anymore. He slowly backed toward the door and unlocked the deadbolt. He darted his eyes back and forth between the door and the sheriff, until he reached back to for the door handle, planning to see if Julie was truly in the Marshport Police car.

Like a coiled viper, the sheriff lunged forward as soon as Damon dropped his guard. He forced the end of the gun toward the floor and drove the crown of his forehead down to the bridge of Damon's nose.

Damon's eyes watered as the perimeter of his vision closed in white. He stumbled but pulled everything within him to stay on his feet. As he centered himself, the realization set in. The sheriff now had his gun.

Sheriff Mason slid out the clip and flicked the bullets from it one by one, each of them sounding off a metallic click and they flew out. He walked closer to Damon.

"You know I have it well within my rights to shoot you now in self-defense? You aimed a live firearm at an officer of the law. But I'm not gonna do that. Not yet." He whipped Damon in the ear with the pistol, knocking him to the ground.

As Damon lay helpless on the carpet, the world spun around him. His eyes still watering. His ears ringing. His mind raced as he struggled to breathe. He imagined it felt much like drowning.

"I know you can still hear me, Mr. Williams," Mason said, that confident condescension returning in full force. "So, I need you to listen close before you do something reckless. Tonight, admittedly, hasn't gone how I intended." He chuckled and sucked his front teeth in an audible smack. "You just gotta keep picking away at stuff, don't ya? But you're smart. You gotta know, there's only a few ways out of this. One, dead. Obviously. Killed by the brave Marshport sheriff protecting his town from a sick-minded vigilante with wild theories. God, I'd be a hero. Two, under arrest for the murder of Kirk Jameson. Town staple. Son of a founding member of the Marshport Historical Society. Loved by all. Or three, you can join us."

Damon let out a guttural groan as he climbed back to his feet. "Never! Take me to Adam. He better be alive or—"

"See? I knew you were still with us," Mason said, cutting him off. He ran his finger up and down the wood paneling covering the walls as he walked, weaving it in and out of the knickknacks and framed newspaper clippings of town milestones. "Son, I've been trying to enlighten you off the rip. We're getting older, as you can plainly see. We need a new generation. For the good of the town. For it to thrive. Why do you think I sent you all over to meet people? Get ingrained in the community? You've met my officers. They're good enough, but not really the leadership type. But you? I saw something in you right away." He stopped at an oil painting of an angel holding the arm of an elderly man with a knife. The sheriff grimaced and shook his head. "You'd be thrust in a bit sooner than I would have hoped, so I understand the friction, here. But, trust me, once you see it for yourself, I swear. I was skeptical, too."

Damon charged at Mason and swung on him, hoping to catch him off guard. The sheriff blocked the first hit with his elbow, but two others connected. Sheriff Mason reeled back and tripped over an end table in the process. He toppled over to the ground. Damon ripped the sheriff's handcuffs from his belt, but before he could use them, Mason hit him in the chin with an upward swing, knocking him onto his back. The sheriff rested on one knee for a moment before pushing off and standing back up.

"I don't know what your end game is here, son. But I'm not gonna spar with you. We've got things to d—"

Damon spun around and hit Mason in the side of the face with a table lamp. The force crumpled both the flat base and cylindrical body, as the sheriff fell to the ground with a hard, lifeless thud.

Damon knew he'd wasted too much time already. He sprinted throughout the house, looking in the bedrooms and closets. "Adam!" he screamed. "Adam, can you hear me?" He pounded on walls and turned over dressers and bookcases and anything else possibly hiding a hidden passage or a corridor. "Adam!" He ran back through the living room.

The sheriff slowly climbed back to his feet, but Damon ran right past him. Unfortunately, he knew it was his word against Mason's at this point, so having the man dead or even tied up did nothing for him. He heard Mason on the phone. Whatever the hell was going on was happening tonight. He needed something concrete, and fast.

In the kitchen, Damon flung open a door to find stairs leading down to the basement. He looked around for a light switch before seeing a small ceiling light with a string hanging from it. He pulled the string with slightly too much force, given the adrenaline rush, and it snapped where the dry-rotted cord met up to a small chain. "Shit," he said as he whipped it aside. Damon reached up and pinched the chain with his thumb and index finger. When he pulled, the wooden stairs illuminated in a soft amber glow.

He pulled out his phone and scrolled through contacts, trying to find someone to call for assistance. As he stepped forward to descend, Damon was yanked backward by his jacket hood. He clipped the kitchen island with his side and spun around, falling on the broken shards from the glass Kirk had dropped what felt like forever ago. His phone flew from his grip and slid across the kitchen floor until it hit the wall. Sheriff Mason pressed his knee in between Damon's shoulder blades and dug the tip of his gun into the back of his head.

"Boy, I'm done. Don't make me shoot you right here in this kitchen. It will draw a lot of attention. We'll get calls about people hearing gunshots. And it would be an even bigger mess, which I'd have to clean up. And I would. Now you know you ain't leaving. Not if you think there's a chance you can get to that boy. Which, I know you can't fathom, but you'd be doing him a disservice. Pulling him from the light."

"You led the fucking investigation," Damon said.

"I had you chasin' your tail is what I was doing. Private investigator." Mason scoffed. "In my town? You had me nervous a bit, that's for sure. Just couldn't leave well enough alone. I told 'em! Now get up. I know you well enough already. The need to know is eating you alive at this point. I promise you, once you see it with your own eyes, it'll change everything."

Damon complied, knowing the sheriff was unfortunately right about him. Sheriff Mason led him down the creaky wooden stairs to the basement. When they reached the bottom, it smelled of concrete and cobwebs and dust. The basement was empty, except for stacks of cardboard boxes, the contents of which were written in black marker on the sides. A furnace and water heater. A washer. A dryer. And a metal door.

The door stood nearly seven feet high, and the dull and dented metal looked like it had been in place for decades. It had no knob, just a vertical curved handle. A heavy-duty brass padlock hung from a clasp above the handle. Sheriff Mason forced Damon against the wall beside the door.

"Don't move," he said. "At this point, I will not hesitate to put a bullet in your fucking head." He pulled a key ring from his belt and flipped through until finding what he needed. As he slid the key into the lock, he took a breath and whispered to himself. "Paul, they're getting you all worked up. Got ya cussin'. Getting your blood pressure all up."

He gave the door a hearty tug, and it opened with a drawn-out, grinding cry as the hinges twisted against each other. As Sheriff Mason pulled the key and hung the padlock back to the clasp, Damon sprang. He slammed the sheriff's hand against the side of the door, and the gun flew from his grip, bouncing on the ground.

Sheriff Mason seized Damon by the throat with both meaty hands, forcing him backward. As he constricted Damon's neck, he inched forward step by step. Damon struggled to loosen the grip. He hammered down on the sheriff's hands with his own fist, but they only dug in harder. The two hit the washing machine, upending the feet as Damon bent over backward on the corner of it, trying and failing to peel the sheriff's hands from his throat. With gritted teeth and crazed eyes, Mason stared down at Damon.

"I tried to give you a choice," he growled. "They tried to just get you out of town. Why can't you accept what is best for this child? And for you?"

Damon pulled his hand into his coat sleeve and came back out gripping a chunk of the broken drinking glass hidden inside. He thrust it upward and jammed it into the sheriff's neck, just below his jaw.

Mason reeled backward, holding the wound on the side of his neck. Damon charged toward him, pushing him to stagger faster until he hit the cinder-block wall with a smack. Damon screamed as he stabbed him again in the throat, then in the ribs. He squeezed the chuck of glass so tightly as he stuck Sheriff Mason again and again, he didn't know how much of the blood covering his hands was the sheriff's or his own.

As Mason fell lifeless to the ground, Damon collapsed next to him. He wanted to scream and pass out simultaneously. His entire body shook and ached as he closed his eyes and allowed the cool cement basement floor to soothe him, even if just for a moment.

Upstairs, the front door opened, and Damon's ears perked up as someone audibly gasped, presumably after stumbling upon Kirk's body. The slow, uneven footsteps echoed through the floors into the basement, reverberating off the walls into the open space. As they approached the top of the stairs, he panicked and shot up. Damon looked around before scrambling beside the cardboard boxes and crouching beside them. The footsteps somehow fell quieter the farther down the stairs the person descended, until she fully appeared into view.

"Julie," Damon said, equally excited and relieved. "Oh, thank god."

"Damon?" Her jaw dropped. "What's going on? I was waiting for the sheriff and heard crashing. I came in and Kirk and— oh shit are you okay?"

"I'm okay. It's not my blood." He looked down his front. "Most of it at least."

Julie's entire body trembled and she shot her arms down at her side."Damon, what the fuck is going on?"

He looked at the sheriff lying on the ground and could no longer keep it together. "I still don't really know. But they're . . . they're all in on it, Julie. Whatever it is. They have him. They're—"

His focus was seized by hymnal music and a faint orange light at the end of the tunnel beyond the door. He looked to Julie once more, who appeared drawn to it as well. That face. He could tell. She knew as well as he did, they had to head through that door right now.

Damon grabbed the flashlight from Sheriff Mason's belt and picked up the revolver from the dusty tunnel entrance. He checked the chamber.

"Full," he said to her, and flicked his wrist to close it. "Here." He handed Julie the piece of broken glass, which he'd still been gripping in his hand. It pulled at the skin as he separated it from his palm to hand it over.

Cautiously, side by side, they entered the tunnel.

CHAPTER THIRTY-EIGHT

The tunnel was made up of thick wooden beams, red bricks, and loose stones covered in mortar. Long, interconnected strings of unlit overhead lights were fixed to the top of the wall along the way. With no time to discover how they powered on, Julie let Damon walk half a step ahead of her, lighting their path with the flashlight. The entire time, she fought the urge to sprint as fast as she could down the hall.

They slowly followed the singing until they reached an open, circular room. The passage they exited appeared to be one of four tunnels that dead-ended into it. Oil lamps made of glass, fixed to the walls around the perimeter, provided enough light to navigate the room but didn't illuminate more than a couple of feet into the other passages.

The space's centerpiece was a stone slab raised on a brick base roughly four feet tall, its edges all chipped and worn with age. At the head of the slab stood two unlit torches perched on full-sized metal spiraling bases. Between them, facing the slab, stood an altar. A small mask of what appeared to be a ram, or a goat, sat on a bust resting on the altar. Next to it, nested in a wooden display holder, was a curved steel dagger with a dark green handle.

Julie held back tears as she circled the display, inspecting it.

"What are these sick fucks up to?"

"I wish I knew." Damon nodded to a painting hanging from the alter. "I've seen similar art displayed around town." It showed an angel with a ram in its arms descending from heaven. The angel looked to be stopping an elderly man who towered over a boy on a formation similar to the one in front of them. "I just thought it was shitty taste, at first. Now I'm getting goosebumps just looking at it."

As they studied the mural, the echoed singing grew louder. One of the connecting passages began to glow. Damon pulled Julie back into where they had recently exited, and knelt in the shadows.

"What are you doing?" she snapped at him. "We need to push forward."

"I know. We don't know what we're up against. And they don't know we're here. We need that advantage."

Julie knew he was right, but she hated it. The back of her neck throbbed; it felt like every pulse was counting down the time she was rapidly running out of. She bounced nervously as the singing made its way into the circular room.

A line of figures in black, hooded robes emerged from the passageway, marching in synchronized steps into the ceremony room. The one at the head carried an open book and sang the ritualistic melody. Two followed behind with lit candles. As they filed in, Julie stopped counting when her throat closed in on itself. Seeing the end of the procession, her insides constricted and she nearly vomited.

Four of the figures, one at each corner, carried what resembled a medical stretcher, constructed with elaborately finished wooden poles and held together by a decorative purple cloth. On the cloth of the stretcher rested a young boy who lay somewhere between asleep and awake. His feet were bound with rope, and his hands folded and laid over his chest. Stripped down to his underwear, his malnourished body had a gray hue and showed ribs starting to push against the skin.

Though he barely resembled the smiling, sensitive boy she'd lost weeks ago, Julie didn't have to get any closer to know immediately who the transport was.

She covered her mouth to stifle her own scream. "That's him. They have my baby," she said to Damon between a whisper and cry. "I don't see him breathing. Is he breathing? Is he alive?" she asked, knowing Damon didn't have the answers she needed.

"I saw his chest move. I think he's sedated," he said, offering little comfort. He must have seen Julie fighting off hyperventilating, because he took her hand and whispered. "We're getting him out of here. But there's too many of them to just rush in. I need you to trust me."

The robed group took their position, stopping at the foot of the slab, before the front one took his spot at the head of the altar.

"We ask the acolytes to light the Fires of Binding and invite God to see forth that we are true and pure and devout," the man said.

He had a tall, broad figure and a proper voice that didn't quite match his size. It was recognizable to Julie, but she couldn't put a finger on where from. It didn't matter. She was going to kill him soon. She suddenly tasted blood, and realized she'd been biting down on her lip so hard she'd broken the skin.

The two hooded figures walked along either side of the stone bed and slowly raised their candlesticks to the torches. The torches sparked in a small glowing ball, then expanded to a steady, flickering flame. The two paused at the altar, bowed their heads in respect, and fanned out to the wall, where they hung the candelabras and returned to their place.

The look on Damon's face—Julie could tell he was trying to piece together what was happening and form some sort of strategy. But how complicated could it be? Shoot as many as they could until the gun ran dry, stab a few others, grab Adam and run. She envisioned herself rushing out to save him, only to be stopped and killed herself. Adam was so close, but somehow still felt like a chasm lay between them. Like if she reached out to touch him, his fingertips would forever be just slightly out of reach.

"And now, with your guidance, we present to you our sacrifice."

"Sacrifice? What do they mean 'sacrifice'?" Julie said to Damon. "We have to go."

He put his hand on her shoulder but didn't outright answer her.

With two members on each side, they carefully moved Adam from the transport to the stone slab. They fixed his arms over his chest and propped his head to face straight to the ceiling.

"Our town is blessed. Blessed by God for the offering which we make in his name. Like the blessings brought to the people by Abraham's unwavering devotion. The willingness to sacrifice his son in the name of the Lord, only to have the angels stop him and exchange for a ram in the boy's stead." The speaker slid the ram mask over Adam's face. "The offering is no longer the spawn of the nonbeliever, but is transformed into the sacrificial ram. For our Father, we make this offering in exchange for your blessings upon our town and our people. We live for your word, your light, and your love. In your name."

"Fuck," Damon whispered to himself as he leaned over to Julie. "We're out of time. I need you to stay here. If anything happens to me, grab Adam and run."

The man grabbed the dagger from its display on the altar, and Damon shot up out of the shadowed tunnel exit.

"Stop!" Damon yelled. He aimed the gun at the one with the dagger, shifting his attention from person to person. "Don't move. Drop the knife!"

"Damon? How did you get down here? Where is Sheriff

Mason?" the cloaked figure asked. He sounded more inconvenienced than anything else.

"I said drop it! Move and I will shoot you."

"Mr. Williams, listen to me. I know your intentions are noble, but you don't know what you're doing," he said as he lowered the blade onto the altar beside him. "What you're up against. What is at stake here."

"Who are you people? Show yourselves!" Damon said.

The one with the knife slowly reached up to the hood covering his face and pulled back, revealing himself to be Gregory Calhoune. He looked at the others and nodded. They removed their hoods as well, revealing Sherri, Gloria, and the rest of the Marshport Historical Society.

"Gregory? Wha . . . what the hell is this?"

"It is our duty, Mr. Williams. The boy must be offered. The Lord sent him to us in order to be saved. And in return, our town can continue to flourish and be blessed."

"You did this? You're all in on it? Everyone knows?" Damon asked. It came out more as stream of consciousness than actual questions. His attention stayed focused on the group, though all color bled from his face and he looked physically ill.

Julie felt she might actually get sick here in this dark corner underground. Her body quaked, and she held back everything within her screaming to rush out, kill them all, and grab her son.

Gregory laughed and shook his head. "Oh, don't be daft," he said, and gestured outward. "We protect the town. From themselves, really. However, everyone does need to bring the right mindset for the community to work. They know they're blessed, and don't ask questions about how."

The information seemingly hit Damon in chunks as he processed.

"Oh, my God. So, Ava . . . and Dillon? You just . . ." He lowered his head for a second.

"Romans 12:2, Mr. Williams," Gregory said.

Gloria stepped forward. "'And be not conformed to this world, but be ye transformed by the renewing of your mind. That ye may prove what is that good, and acceptable, and perfect, will of God.'" She stepped forward once more toward Damon. "He sent the fires that cleansed our town and showed us the path back to him. It was always the lost children. I tried telling Sheriff Mason you wouldn't grasp the gravity of our mission."

Julie dry-heaved as the revelation convulsed in her stomach. "You're fucking monsters," she blurted out from the shadows, and emerged from cover holding the chunk of glass out in front of her. She inched closer to Damon and waved the makeshift weapon back and forth at the group.

"Mrs. Newcommer?" Gregory said. His flash of confusion seemed to quickly settle into acceptance. "Well, you're not supposed to have to witness the ceremony, but it changes nothing. Although, this will be the first with multiple offerings."

"Do you hear yourself? You murder children!" Julie said.

"We would never!" Gloria scoffed. "Not in the eyes of God, we aren't. They're not even his children." She raised her arms to the sky. "We are delivered the children of nonbelievers and followers of sacrilegious lifestyles. It is our burden to offer them to the Lord. Send them home so they can be baptized in his love, and in return, our town is blessed in his light. No one enjoys this. Not for the faint of heart. But we take on the responsibility. It is our duty. And we will not allow you to stand in our way and jeopardize our community and way of life."

"You self-righteous fucks think you decide what's right and wrong?" Julie said.

"You think we take joy in this?" Gregory said. He somehow looked surprised. "It's not up to us."

"Don't move," Damon said. "I'm taking Adam."

A line of them formed a shield between the slab and Damon and Julie.

"We can't let you do that, child," Sherri said. "We aren't the bad guys here. We are saving them. Saving them from a life of wandering aimlessly. Lost without a guiding light. Look inside. You know it to be true."

They closed in on Damon and Julie, and Damon fired. Gloria's head snapped back. She stumbled briefly and folded to the ground. The sound of the shot echoed throughout the room and down the tunnels. All the others stopped and winced at the blast before noticing Gloria on the ground, blood running from the hole in the middle of her forehead.

"I warned you. Get back!" Damon said.

They retreated slowly, and Julie ran to Adam. She wrapped the ceremonial cloth around the boy, who lay before them, barely conscious.

Sherri and Gregory approached.

"You don't know what you're doing. I don't think you fully grasp what's at stake here," Sherri said. "This is a crucial part of the Marshport way of life."

Damon whipped around. "I said get the fuck back!" He hovered beside Julie, keeping the others at bay while she checked on her son.

Julie lightly tapped his cheeks and laid her head next to his face to check for breathing. "Adam. Adam, can you hear me? We're going to get you out of here. Mommy's here."

"You're not listening to us," Gregory said, from behind them. They missed him break from the rest, and he now stood behind them with the dagger raised above his head.

As he plunged down, Damon covered Julie and Adam, and the blade drove into his right shoulder. He cried out and reeled backward. Gregory used his boot to force him away from the cement table. Damon tumbled to the dirt as he reached back, attempting to grasp the blade. But it was just out of reach.

As Gregory watched Damon falter, Julie felt the others

approaching her. She turned and attacked with the chunk of glass. She swiped at the face of one and couldn't tell if she hit the eye or just below it, but they covered their face and recoiled. She stuck another twice in the stomach. Then another, but they caught her arm and drove her head backward onto the edge of the slab. She bounced off and smacked face-first into the dirt as at least two people held her down.

She yelled for Damon, trying to warn him, as Gregory walked up and kicked him again in the abdomen, knocking him back over. As he wailed and writhed, he was finally able to grab the handle and pull the knife from his shoulder. Gregory stepped on the open wound, reaching down to pry the blade from Damon's grip. Two group members knelt on Damon's back, holding him on the ground.

"Oh, he is really testing us this time," Gregory said. "I can only think Kirk's mishap with our last offering is to blame for it."

Pinned to the ground, Julie looked up at the ceremonial bed on which her son lay. Her son, who'd never know how hard she fought to save him. Never know how close she got. She realized Stephen would go on probably thinking both his parents killed themselves from the grief. A lie he'd have weighing on him his entire life.

"I tried telling you all at the time that the girl wouldn't suffice without the ceremony. But you didn't listen," Sherri said.

"Which is why he's making our offering this time so sizable," Gregory said. He stood over Adam with the dagger held in his interlocking hands.

"No!" Julie screamed into the ground. Spit and tears misted the air as the guttural growl shook her, but she went nowhere. Her eyes and throat burned as she collapsed and turned her head away, seeing the defeated, sorrowful, apologetic face of Damon.

He locked eyes with her, and something in his look

changed. His eyes narrowed, and he drove his knuckles into the ground.

As Gregory slowly raised the blade above his head, he said, "We live for your word, your light, and your love. We offer this in your name."

Damon threw his head back and smacked it against the face of the person holding him down. He shot up and grabbed one of the torch stands from beside the altar and stuck Gregory in his chest with the butt of it, knocking him backward. Gregory doubled over, and Damon did it once more, screaming as he drove him backward him into the wall.

Gregory collided with one of the glass oil lamps, which shattered upon impact. Oil and flames covered him, catching his robes ablaze. He flailed and reached back, grasping at the cloak to try and rip it off as the flames spread around and over him. The sound of his cries along with the roaring flames stole everyone's attention.

The remaining group members all rushed to him, pulling their own robes off to snuff out the flames on his back. Pockets of burning oil scattered on the ground around them.

Julie swore she could smell the skin already cooking and blistering as his body fused with the fabric. She took half a second to watch the man burn before rushing to Adam. Wrapping him up in the cloth he lay on, and lifting him from the slab, she held him and wept.

"Julie, run!" Damon yelled.

She headed toward the tunnel they'd entered from, but the Marshport Historical Society members stood in the way, attending to Gregory.

Damon hurled the torch he still held at an oil lamp on the opposite wall. Flame erupted around them, blinding them in the surging, heated flash. Damon turned and pulled another from the wall behind him. He threw it at the ceiling above the historical society members. The fire grew enough to separate Julie and him from the others.

"C'mon!" Damon said as he ran through the closest opening.

Julie followed closely behind, with Adam in tow. The passage was long and dark, but they kept running, Damon's flashlight bouncing erratically and barely guiding the way. As they continued down the passageway, Julie looked behind periodically but saw nothing besides the orangish-red glow of the fiery ceremony room.

They blindly ran until they almost ran face-first into a narrow metal spiral staircase. Without hesitation, they climbed the winding stairs and came to a door in the tunnel ceiling. Damon turned the oversized sash lock and pushed the ceiling door open with his shoulder.

Julie stepped over the ledge at the top of the stairs and into a pitch-black room. Damon shined the flashlight around, and they searched for any sort of identifying marks. It smelled like incense and fabric softener. She rested against the wall, finally feeling okay to catch her breath. She felt her heart beating slower as the adrenaline began to wane. The cold air from the tunnel brushed up against the back of her neck, causing the fine hairs to stand on end.

Though Julie couldn't see much of anything, Damon visibly sank as his eyes locked on the wall opposite of where they stood.

"No," he said as he shuffled over to it. He leaned his head against the wall, and Julie finally spotted a decent-sized hole broken through the middle.

Without looking, Damon reached up and grabbed a handle Julie hadn't even noticed. He pulled the latch and gave an assertive tug. His shoulder looked like it screamed as the stab wound stretched and separated, but he didn't seem to care. The door clicked and swung toward him.

Julie followed Damon through as he kicked a vacuum cleaner and another box of something out of the way. He turned the knob, stumbling out of the closet and into the hallway of the O'Leary house.

Corrine sat on the couch in the living room. Alone and in the dark, seemingly entranced by an electric fireplace and her own thoughts. She jumped at the crashing coming from the hallway.

"Help!" Damon yelled.

"Oh my god! Is that Adam? Where did you . . . Oh my god."

"We need help, now! Call an ambulance!"

Corrine grabbed her phone and walked back and forth frantically, trying to process. "I'll—I'll call the sheriff," she said.

"No!" Julie and Damon said in unison.

"I'll explain when we can," Damon said. "But no one from Marshport. We need to get Adam to a hospital."

With Adam tightly wrapped in her arms, Julie melted into the couch. She kissed him and smelled him and kissed him again. "It's him," she said. "It's really him."

"Careful," Damon said. "He's weak."

"I know. I know. I just . . . I never gave up, baby. You need to know that. I never gave up," Julie whispered into his ear. She shot her attention to the other two. "He—he needs the hospital. Where's the fucking ambulance?"

"They're on their way now, babe," Corrine said. "Be here soon."

Shortly after, emergency medical response arrived, as well as state police. Damon's uncle's connections on the force arrived swiftly and offered people they could trust. Damon told them everything, including about the other children and what they'd had to do to escape the tunnels with Adam. The officers split into different directions, some headed straight into the hall closet. Others rushed off to Kirk's address.

As Adam was wheeled into the back of the ambulance, Julie followed along in step with one hand on the cart and the other holding her son's hand. She gripped the rail until she had to let go and allow him to slide through the rear double doors. She climbed inside and crouched beside him, where she stayed the entirety of the way to the hospital.

CHAPTER THIRTY-NINE

Damon walked through the parking lot toward the sliding front doors of Torwood General Hospital. A gust of wind kicked, and he grabbed the half of his coat draped over the shoulder currently in a sling, pulling it tight against him. The cold snap of the Ohio early winter finally took hold, and the blacktop wisped with pockets of light, dusty snow.

He knocked on the door to Adam's room and poked his head inside. Julie sat at her son's bedside—he was sitting up and eating a hamburger and a fruit cup from the cafeteria. Stephen sat on the other side of the hospital bed, reading comics. Corrine stood behind Julie, scratching her back. She noticed Damon first and tapped Julie on the shoulder, pointing to the private investigator standing in the doorway.

"Damon!" Julie said. "Come in. Please."

He nervously shuffled into the room as Julie stood up and met him halfway. She went in for a hug, but after noticing his injury just rubbed his arm.

"Oh, don't worry about it. I'm fine. Should get all the stitches out in a few days. How is he?" he asked, shifting his eyes toward Adam.

"He's doing so much better. Still getting his weight and energy back. But he's been out of bed, getting around with assistance. He should be up and out of a wheelchair soon. He was just moved from the ICU to this room yesterday."

"That's great," he said. He stuttered a bit, wondering how or if he should ask about what else was at the forefront of his mind. "And how are they, or really all of you . . . I mean, do they know?"

"Of course. But I don't think with everything it's fully sunk in for them yet. But we've talked. Mostly Stephen and I, while staying here. The funeral is Monday. I just keep replaying everything, and I don't know . . ." She trailed off, biting her bottom lip and swallowing hard. "If he didn't go to that house that night, I don't know if we ever—God. He was taken from us because he got too close to finding our son. In a twisted, bittersweet way, we're trying to keep that in perspective."

"Mrs. Newcommer, I'm so sorry. If I would've worked faster, or smarter, it wouldn't have happened. I still can't stop thinking of all the things I missed. I blame myself."

"Stop. You're a hero, Damon. Please understand that."

"Oh, no. I'm no hero. I was just doing my job. That's actually—it's one reason I came by. With everything that happened, I can't take this." From his coat pocket, Damon slipped out a yellow, folded-up manila envelope containing the down payment the Newcommers had given him at the diner when they met. "Please. It doesn't feel right."

"Damon, don't," she said, blocking the envelope and pushing his arm down. She smiled and glanced back at the boys before looking at Damon again. "Come here a minute," she said. She pulled him closer to the bed.

"Boys, you guys haven't officially met. This is Damon Williams. We have him to thank for everything."

Damon shot a glance at her, then back to the boys. "Oh, really I—"

"Mom said you saved me," Adam said. His voice was scratchy but upbeat. His body was attached to various monitors and an IV, but his color and appearance looked much better than the child he'd pulled from below Marshport not long ago. "I don't really remember, but she told me some."

Damon choked up and stuffed his hand into his pocket. "Of course," he said. "I'm so happy I could."

"I saw you on the news," Stephen said. "Are you sure they got them all?"

"I mean, I believe so. At least the ones who were—"

Julie leaned her head back and raised her eyebrows.

"Yeah," Damon said. "They got them all."

"Boys, I'm gonna step out and talk to Damon real quick. Okay?" Julie said.

They exited into the hall and closed the door.

"Sorry. Adam is still scared they're going to come back for him."

"That's terrible," Damon said. "They did get everyone who was down in the tunnels. The sick bastards didn't even fight it. Still claimed they were doing the Lord's work and saving the children, even while in custody. But Julie, there's no way of knowing how far that went in Marshport. I'm no hero. Someone contacted me about writing a book telling what happened. News stations keep calling me for interviews. It all feels gross."

"You saved my son's life and took out the monster that murdered my husband. The parents of the other children can finally have closure. We owe you everything. Of course you're taking the money. You're also going to take the rest of the payment, as well. As for the other stuff, well, I can't help you with that. But it's been close to a week, and I still find myself tearing up every time I hear Adam's voice."

Damon's eyes reddened, and he shook his head.

"I'm going to go back in," Julie said. "You're more than welcome to come in and stay as long as you like."

"No, no. I'm happy to see him doing well. But I should go."

She smiled and rubbed his arm again before returning to the hospital room.

Back in his car and on the highway, Damon followed I90 heading back toward Cleveland. For much of the drive, he tried to ignore the impulse that had been eating away at him. Ever since that night, he'd thought about almost nothing except for that rabbit hole, and its depth. As he approached the upcoming interchange, it called out to him like a siren's song. The need to know consumed him.

He glanced behind him, then flicked his signal to take the exit and head south toward Marshport.